TALES OF
THE BAJA

T. Palos

authorHOUSE®

AuthorHouse™
1663 Liberty Drive
Bloomington, IN 47403
www.authorhouse.com
Phone: 833-262-8899

Published by AuthorHouse 04/11/2023

ISBN: 979-8-8230-0267-7 (sc)
ISBN: 979-8-8230-0265-3 (hc)
ISBN: 979-8-8230-0266-0 (e)

Library of Congress Control Number: 2023904088

Print information available on the last page.

CONTENTS

FREE PREVIEWS

He went down that day... then out- "GONE!". Not put down, like, "taken out by another," be it a bullet or an irate vehicle. Not taken out of this Earthly existence, like, returned to the Lord in fondness of his of his old age. NO, he went away 'Surf-riding' with his life to the end of his time.

He was not sure to believe his eyesight. After all, it's 7:00 am and he has 'jet-lag' from the three day trip to get to this desolate god forsaken place. A skinny, weathered, leather-skinned man in an old, sun-bleached and holey-frayed 'Dewey Weber' t-shirt, wearing dated trunks and 'flip-flops; "this is my uncle?" A Nephew would think the man would have more respect for himself.

KEY NOTE

Remember it's fiction.

Remember – this is one short book of a trilogy.

Call me full of... nonsense. Tell me you don't believe it. As one that doesn't believe in the 'Green-Flash'.. Until you see it personally.

This is how one should read and absorb the Tales from T. Palos.

This was written for people to escape the boredom and repetition of the real everyday life.

The blurred pictures are a reflection of the well used mind of T. Palos as his recollection of long ago fades.

The Tales presented on these pages are loosely arrainged from stories and events that I've collected and remember in my mind during my lifetime and wanted to put together before I forget with 'old-timers' disease.

I hope you will escape the box and enjoy the Tales as much as I did in presenting them.

Thank you Christopher Stone, JRR Tolkien, Herman Melville, Steinbeck, Hemingway, Miguel De Cervantes, and the many others, for sending my mind away from TV in the evening and night hours of my youth.

CHAPTER 1

A Requiem of A Legend

He went down that day... -then out- "GONE!" Not put down, like, taken out by another, weather it be a bullet or an irate vehicle. Not taken out of this earthly existence, like, returned to the lord in fondness of his old age. No, he went away surf riding with his life, to the end.

I was there-

It was a fine clean edged ride. I watched from the take off through the point, when the golden ray of the sun shot across the water and joined the tubing, cresting lip, meeting in a golden rainbow, engulfing his board and him. I watched the wave turn and whip itself into the fine-edged race way and plume into a rainbow of all colors imaginable, twice it's size. I watched the warm Chubasco off shore wind blow the wave back out to sea and thus dissolve into unseen molecules.

Dissipating 'Red' also.

I caught the next wave. It rose and broke the same. It was around 6', enough for a slight squat 'quasi-moto' stance, leaning on my left foot with my calf muscle and thy for speed. And I pulled out 1/4 of a mile down the beach. The point was a solid corduroy scene of waves, maybe 13 perfectly spaced waves. Each breaking as perfect as the next.

I looked in both directions along the shoreline twice, Red was gone! Maybe he just never pulled out. My life was not the same after that. Nothing miraculous, because there have been other pivotal moments. No, it's more about focus, what's important. Did I age or become ageless?

Life that was accepted as important and responsible was not a reality to me anymore. I guess my life hadn't been 'normal' for some time and now I began to accept it. What's important... I'm talking about the years I devoted to preparation for the dream- then to make it real. I guess some people, like the super-ego surf-pros know, well, do they realize, I mean the truth, what we surf riders do?

Can I describe it, being a 'Surfer'? With a word... fantastic. Much of the rider's drama is not seen, it is felt, which boarders on not real to most people. There is a surf song and the only word spoken is 'surfing'. It's a long-boarder's song. Scientifically, surfing is connecting, riding, Cosmic energy.

Some local Mexican fisherman found Red as they were beach combing for lost buoys a day after the three day swell. We drove his 1947 Buick Roadmaster Estate four wheel drive Woody down the beach at low tide to pick him up. Of course 'Tex Ludie' complained about having to buy the gas. We said, "Well why did you buy it?" We knew the answer, he always paid for gas because he had no vehicle. Tex Ludie is doing good now, as far as finances are concerned. He gets $700 a month social security from the United States, deposited in a Mexican bank called 'Banco De Surfen' in a town about two hours away. He retired too soon, and it equates to a low to moderate lifestyle here.

He didn't look too bad, Red that is. No crushed head. A few fingers and toes were eaten off and encrustations were moving into a lot of his orifices. I didn't look everywhere, he still had his crimson surf trunks on. That should be good for some manufacturer's add-

"Stays on even to the death"!

Everybody who was anybody in Reds life as far as we knew was there, so we decided to do the deed, the right of passage from this realm, right then and there. Besides, no one wanted to lift him up. Dapper went back to town in the 1950 Jeep Wagoneer to tell the news and get beer and provisions for three days, the length of time we would have with a chest of iced down brew. Oh yes, this was going to be a proper surfer's send off!

2

Can I describe it? Surfing; what we do? What about sound... the steady drowning hum. You know, some know, moms know- the sound that puts their babies to sleep. Even the sound makes people tired. A surfer first must hear the earths cosmic hum then practice to be strong and not tire in order to push farther into the energy. Out to sea, that energy can screech and howl and roar as in a hurricane. We surfers are attracted to these sea-spawned typhoon melodies.

I rode my first hurricane with Red. It was 1967 I think. He was known as 'Fin-First-Fudge' back then on account of his antics in a crowd of surfers. He liked to paddle into a wave, the bigger the better, fin first and do a helicopter 180 degree spin of his board down the face of the wave before doing a bottom turn in front of a group of wide-eyed surfers. I didn't know him personally then, but anyone from the area knew his style. We were surfing 'Trestles' and the waves were averaging in sets of three to six waves. Our long boards were shorter than the wave faces, there was still two more feet above the wave on the bottom turn. I watched 'The Fudge' take off four yards farther out than the pack. He stood up quick and turned high, hard and with a full long-board rail, with his back foot maybe six inches in front and on top of his single fin. By the time the offshore wind plume spray began to form up the face of the wall of wave, he had already walked jaguar like to the nose of his board and, just to show that he could, he hung half of his left foot and all five of his toes over the nose of the board. He carved his line outside the first three guys. He pulled his foot back and used both feet to hold about thirty inches of front inside rail up high, far in front of the curl. Oh the sound of the crashing wave hissing rhythmically! The heaving breath of some seven surfers paddling hard to get over the top of the oceans surge, and maybe make it out to one of the other set waves, and yes there it was, the incessant drone from mother earth's womb. There was a 'whop' sound and the spray from 'Red's most incredible turn as he changed rails and direction in a full rail carve. His Jacobs three 1/4 inch redwood stringered, 9' 8" Phil Edwards shaped craft, with the red rails, put a bit of cautioned panic in those who seemed to be in his way. He always had red boards and later earned the right to wear red trunks. And then there was the sound of those waves that day... like a huffing freight train inching up a valley as the salty lip peeled from top to bottom. He was far out in front of that curl.

I followed his every move that day and hence my position for the next wave in the set was impeccable. I tried to concentrate on my take-off and stand up but the noise from his wave and the one behind mine was brutally distracting. First, there was the hiss of the plume and Red's fin spray changed the color and texture of the sea which blew back onto the face of my wave making my take-off blind, as if I was in a rain storm, and there was the freight train rhythmic thunder as sections of the two feet thick wave lip pitched and fell seven feet to the bottom of the wave face, moving ever closer as I paddled into and dropped down the wall of ocean.

'New Zealanders', the meanest of all swells. They come far. They're generated in the Antarctic and are most dangerous. The swells in the Southern Hemisphere can reach to the heavens 45 feet high. What makes them dangerous as far as surfers are concerned, is when they reach a South facing shore, they act as a grinder. Traveling North in long lines, each undulation sucks out the coarse rocks and vegetation along the shoreline and tumbles them into ever finer grains, taking out and depositing life's basic minerals. 'The Trestles' surf break has 4" cobble rocks in its shore line undulation, acting and being grinding mandibles as the water currents flowed through them in all directions. It's not a place to be walking at a high tide even if you are wearing shoes, which surfers rarely do because they want to feel their feet in the atmosphere as much as possible. Sandals are excepted. A sneaker wave can pull a person off their feet into it's now exposed rocky grinders dragging any living thing to a drowning death and bury the carcass as a ground wooden stick under a fresh layer of sand and gravel until there is nothing left but molecules. The 'New Zealanders' favorite food is seaweed. I've watched it chew a pile of the vegetation bigger than me like a cow munching it's cud and turning the tide water around it the color of tobacco. The seaweed mix makes a glue that the sand sticks to. Other sea life devour the glue depleting it in time for the next Southern Hemisphere cycle. We surfers like to think we are gaining good Karma, and thus rights to ride the waves, by cleaning out the toxic waste not needed in the primordial soup.

4

Surfing providence has been pretty good to us and Red. This time his board washed up with him even though he never used a leash. That was a reason why he quit surfing professionally. It was required to strap a cord from ankle to the board during contests. He felt that it was too easy to make a mistake and loose one's board and not have to swim for retrieval. He felt more connected to his shaped craft. The craft was missing the fin. It was ripped off clean from above the center redwood stringer. Too bad it was a sun-rise bonsai with alternating old growth koa and purple heart wood antarsia inlays.

There was plenty of drift wood and dried seaweed around for a fire. Our campfire?.. Well sure, but I'm talking about the 'Big Blaze'. Antonio runs the station de petrol, as well as the closest thing to a hospital in the barrio. 'Dapper' volunteered to go back to town and haul back seven llantas for 'The Fudge'. I thought about it later, he might not know what they were for. Besides, my diction of the dialect in this part of Latin America wasn't that good. Too much Californio gibberish most of the time. Anyways, 'Dapper' wanted his own bed.

"Well..you all either suit up and surf or go home and nurse your ma-mas!" Red always laughed when 'Ludie' said this. He used a John Wayne voice with a strong Texan accent when he said it.

It's evening and its been a long emotional humid day. At least they were on the beach though Red washed up twenty yards from the tide line.

'Dapper' wasn't about to surf out side in the waters in front of a dead man that just washed in. So when Tex gave the battle cry as an excuse to rinse off the day Baja style, he said he would get the seven tires and pay for the gas which saved us the trouble of lagging coins for the two litros of petrol. Maybe Dapper is smart not wanting to submerge in the brine where predators were lurking and smelling the odor of a dead human. I think he wanted a fresh water shower.

"Don't come back smelling like that soap the female surf pro left us." Just to make a point to Dapper, the three of us paddled out just before he left wearing nothing but our speedos. Well, except for 'Ludie', he left his speedos on 'Ole Gnarleys' radio antenna "Bring back paper and gas and mucho matches". "Yeah, like he says, also some mescal, the one in the round bottle".

Dapper cruised slowly up the shoreline and just before he was out of Tex Ludie's eyesight, he flung a pair of speedos and surf trunks into a pile of wet bug flying sea weed and waved.

The round bottle- I had partaken in the imbibing of this distilled agave beverage for the first time with Red. It was in 1975. The Baja Highway One was newly finished which meant the dirt road was now paved from the Tijuana border to the Cabo San Lucas tip.

Red brought his family and a small sail boat skiff. They had two young ones, a boy and a girl ages ten and eight. Red called them, "A perfect cosmic family." His wife was born in Indio California and Red, I think he was French or maybe Bask..Spanish? He says he was born in the Baja and his brother won't say.

Sometimes, after that trip, after that bottle of round-bottle Mescal, I became a true Californio.

We drove all the way to a small town called Loreto and camped for a few days in a bay just South, along the winding Highway 1. The Sea of Cortes sparkled incandescently at night below the nearly full moon. It seemed so unreal, so surreal, I had to ask Red if it was from the influence, from the effects of Mescal. He assured me that what I was seeing was marine microbes. "Flourishing so abundantly in this Baja-Sea of Cortes". We had a full moon eclipse two days later and to this day I've never seen so many stars including several shooting across the depths of the dark night sky. I'm glad I was young then and able to keep those memories for so many years.

I had a 1973 Dodge van and yeah it was furnished hippie style. I built it myself, I installed a sink with running water and a platform bed. There was an India jute carpet and paneled in rosewood veneer plywood. It had eye level sliding windows on both sides custom fit over the sink on one side and above the double doors on the other, in a raised fiberglass roof extension. The inside headliner was a glued on green striped Mexican blanket which looked a lot like the Baja Mexico national flag. The surfboards, there were three custom crafts, hung on racks on the inside. My surf name was derived from this- 'Quien Tres Palos', it was Red's idea. We named the van 'The Voyager Of The Asphalt Seas'. It only had an AM-FM radio, because technology was only to eight tracks and it was too dusty in the Baja for those mechanics. She had air conditioning though, and a built in ice chest that could be removed.

Red had the 47' Buick customized with four wheel drive by a company called Harmon Marmon. It was customized into a vehicle for camping. Both bumpers were shaped meticulously out of the heartwood of old growth red wood from Northern California. There were a few dents in them, he said they made him appear friendly to the indigenous people and indeed he was. Those dents were made from pushing cars in need of repair. On this trip, we stopped on the North Road, the one hundred mile dirt trail from the main highway that leads to the small surf town. We encountered a family stranded on the road, with the hood up on a 50's Oldsmobile. The man was beating on the carburetor float-bowl with a ball-peen hammer, and judging by the indentations on the float-cap it was not the first time he was in this dilemma. Red noticed a frayed wire running across a hot spot and when the fisherman pounded on the car it would shake loose the shorted wire. The hero taped up the wire and gave the family some water and we were on our way. The Legend was a helicopter mechanic in Vietnam in 1964.

Red's family broke up two years later. His wife claimed he spent too much time in the Baja. It was true. The daughter later was killed trying to out run a freight train on a forty yard trestle.

On that trip in 75' I was shown the spot. It was Red's third encounter there.

CHAPTER 2

Turn Over The Seat Cushions Marina We Have Company

He was not sure to believe his eyesight. After all it's 7:00 am and he has jet lag from the three day trip to get to this desolate god forsaken place. A skinny, weathered, leather-skinned man in an old sun bleached and holey frayed Dewey Weber t-shirt wearing dated trunks and flip-flops-this is my uncle? A nephew would think the man would have more respect for himself.

Slim lifts the hood of his 62' jeep wagoner and pulls out a 1/2 pint of, hell, is it tequila or mescal... and a shot glass.

"The bum! Mom was right" Dave says to himself. Slim pours a 1/2 jigger in the ornate shot glass and pours it down the throat of the air filter-less carburetor mounted on the manifold of the 240 cubic inch ford strait six engine. The old surfer quickly jumps into the driver's seat and belch-fire starts the jeep. The uncle jumps out of the driver's seat and shuts the hood and drives to Hernandez's and he buys two liters of petrol part of which he fills back up the half pint bottle under the hood.

"Darn Dave," Slim pulls over to the tall cement curb on the dirt esplanade running along the surf break and leaves the wagoneer running, "I hope I don't embarrass you nephew, but I need to stop by the liquor store and pay my tab." And pick up a round bottle for under the hood he says to himself.

"How long will it take to get out to this place?" asked Dave.

"Not long, but we'll have to spend at least six hours there." Slim takes a bounce from the rutted dusty road down to the sea shore and grins at his nephew. "You see this old jeep only runs twice a day."

Dave curtly explains to his uncle that this would have to change because the Mexican bus returns to the city of La Pas at 11:00 am. It's a five hour drive at best and Dave doesn't know this.

"No Dave you get to stay here for another night. You see, once we stop and turn off the motor in 'Ole Gnarly' here it won't start for six hours." Dave took a large bump badly and hit the inside bare metal roof of the cab with his head which would later give him a neck ache, the bang on the cranium forced him down into the hole between the springs in the truck seat. "Hey, you look a little car sick!" the surfer eases around an incoming shore break.

"Stop, stop!" was now the plaintive cry fifteen minutes of silence later. "Stop the car we have a spider in here!"

"What?" said Slim

"Where?" says the large Tongan woman on the back seat of the wagon. With a creek, she grabs hold with both hands, an enormous one on the passenger seat and the other corpulent one on the driver's seat which causes the old man to swerve the vehicle to gain his balance with the steering wheel, and she sticks her head between them. Her long raven black hair covers both seats and shoulders of the two up front.

"I'll take care of this." She says in her large Tongan accent. There, climbing and then ascending desperately on his web down the radio knob in the dash is indeed a spider. The big right hand deftly, swiftly, and gently, swoops and scoops the arachnid. In one motion she she waves and opens her hand out side of the passenger window. An extra large boob drops over Dave's neck and shoulder.

"Good thing you wore your moo-moo with the top today Marina, Dave might get urges." Dave quickly turns his gaze away and says "Ah she didn't really throw that spider out alive..." "did she?"

Marina is what Slim calls his personal surf-serpa. He had placed an ad on line, well, he had Lunita at the cyber cafe which overlooks second point, set it up about five years ago. The old salt was recovering from a surf injury which limited his ability to carry his 9'6" Greg Knoll 'Dora' cat long board and surf equipment. The blog read something like "serpa needed for three months. Must be able to cook, load and unload supplies and camp out two hundred miles from civilization for the duration. A large island woman preferred." She's twenty years younger than ole Slim and she still carries his stand up board for him with ease. After the three months, which stretched to six months, Slim bought her a ticket home to Tonga as well as a nice wage. He says he missed her octopus ceveche and she says she missed the remote Mexican fishing village. Anyway- she moved back and stayed in his house.

So there they are. About forty five minutes south of the fishing village on the shore of a place called 'bone-yards'. Slim had driven for at least three miles along the tide line in a flock of pelicans. There were at least thirty or maybe twenty birds on both sides of the four wheel drive vehicle. "Darn," he said in his nasally voice, "I was hoping they would let me 'v' squadron with them." Just to have acknowledgment of the wagoneer and still split up on both sides of 'ole gnarly' and allow the surf vehicle to cruise at the same speed as their flight was a rare privilege.

"No 'v' for you bra. They don't trust your driving" said Marina in her husky Tongan voice.

"I think the jeep is too big and the wind draft is too different from the gulls."

"You mean pelicans dad." Joey is in the back compartment of the wagon hanging his hand out the open tailgate window and waving it up and down like a glider in the wind.

"Yeah yeah" says his dad "and how far is this place?"

"Not far, hey Joey, I'm getting tired, how about you drive the rest of the way." Joey is quicker than his dad. "Can a twelve year old drive down here?"

"Sure!" Slim jumps out of 'Ole Gnarley' and the kid is over the seats before Dave answers "Oh... ah, oh.. I don't know?"

"NO one knows. Now we find out." Says the Tongan.

"I'm going to walk awhile." And the old man lets out a fart. "You've got a good teacher there, your Dad."

Dave tries to roll up his window and it gets half way up and the handle comes off in Dave's hand. He quickly puts it back on and rolls down the make shift Plexiglas. "You need a screw for the handle." Slim explains that the door handle thread for the screw is stripped and that he will go 'shopping' to find a wedge-stick to put in it. 'Shopping' - that's what the old surfer calls beach combing.

Joey has his feet on the peddles and pushes on the gas. "Whomph, whomph" belches the exhaust. 'Ole Gnarley' doesn't move and Joey says "Hey, there's three peddles here... well kind of." There's no rubber pads on any of them and they're all warn to a shine. The clutch is warn smooth from years of use and the other two still have their embossed waffle pattern showing shiny. "I've never seen three before."

"And I've never driven with a clutch before" says Dave.

"You're a mechanical engineer. Well thats what Red said you are. You two can figure it out. Remember Joey, don't turn the motor off." Yeah, well how would he know he didn't pay for my engineering degree thought Dave.

"Joey, the car didn't move because the transmission is not engaged." "It's not a car dad it's a surf-wagon. Wow a real one and I'm driving it!" They find the clutch peddle and after a few leaping lizards Joey gets it moving at a pace that Slim can walk and keep up.

"Steer close to the water line but don't go in it," the old uncle instructs. The lad forgets about the tide surge and the brine goes under the tires. Dave gets nervous when they reach a particularly rocky out crop and a tide wave splashes against the door on the passenger side spraying the dad and washing all the way under and over to where it can be seen on the driver's side. "Turn to your left Joey, no left. Pull pull up there in that ravine as far as you can." He does but buries all four wheels down to the axles and the four wheeler stalls. Dave is in a panic and is about to puke, and does, out the window and down the side of the vehicle. Then he finds out the door won't open because the piled up soft sand is higher than the bottom of the door. The jeep is tilted on a sand dune and the dog quickly leaps out the back window and pees on some sea weed. Joey follows the dog and does the same.

"Joey! What are you doing?"

"Uncle Slim did it." The dog saunters over to the passenger door to lick the regurgitation off before the flies find it.

The vehicle groans and begins to tip over on to the passenger side. Marina climbs over the front seat and leans against the driver door and opens it and hangs halfway out of the wagoneer which stabilizes it from rolling over.

"Come here little smart man and climb over Marina's big lap and get out of jeep."

"I can't fit through there!"

"You have to. Come on hurry, I will not hold this position long for you." "There," she says as he slithered under her unshaved arm pit, "you better not brag about having intimate relations with me."

It's then that Dave realizes that the engine is off. "Slim oh no, how long before the car will start?"

"Well, after dark but I don't drive at night." He lied. He planned on staying at 'dead mans' all night anyway. "Oh no' no uncle, we can't stay here all night!" "cool!" says his son.

Marina rolled out on to her back into the soft warm sand. It turned out that the jeep wasn't in as precarious an angle as was perceived and with some digging with the Tongan woman's clam shovel, and some deft steering wheel movement, they pushed the thing to level ground mostly done with the big lady's strength.

"Welcome to 'bone-yards'" grinned Slim in his most mischievous way.

"Four fingers to sundown" says Marina to no one in particular, though all could hear her loud smooth island voice. Holding the fingers below the sun and above the unobstructed horizon is a surfer's way to tell time. And with a bit of French Polynesian in her voice she says "we'll have em halibut camee' for a feast de-zure."

"You have that in the ice chest?" asks Joey.

"I didn't see you load any food" says Dave in his usual skeptic tone of voice. I did see a lot of tacate cans go on the ice."

"Oh we always bring 'thirst aid' when we leave civilization. Says the old leather skinned scrawny surfer. Good thing for bottled water these days. In the old days when me and your dad and the guys first civilized this place all we drank was Mexican coke and beer in cans. The melted ice for water, if we could get it, was contaminated from poor filtration. We saved it for the radiators. Three days, maybe four was about as long as we stayed on uninhabited beaches.

"Ah..alright, you put the white wine in the blanket for safe keeping and now I'll put it on ice. Our meal will be muy equisito." There's a clink sound over the husky voice.

"Here Dave," Slim pulls the tab off the top of a cold cervesa putting it in his nephew hand before he can say no. He pops one for himself and says "it will quiet your stomach." The uncle looks at Joey and then the dad, "that's what your Grandpa Red used to say." He hands Marina a coke and tells her to share it with the kid, he doesn't want to get blamed for giving the youngster too much sugar and he downs half of his beer. So did Dave, which was a mild surprise to everybody. "What's that stuff taste like dad?" "Your too young to know Joey" and Dave sets the half full can on the rear tire.

Marina is busy stushing around the back of the wagoneer with her knees on the tailgate and her ample budier taking up most of the space between the rear compartment pillars. She brings out her clam fork and says "Come on Joey lets dig for the chocolate clams"

He's confused, "chocolate?"

Slim finds his fishing pole and heads for the fingers of lava that jut out to sea as a jetty. There are halibut here and he will catch them on a two inch spinner. No live bait is needed. "Dave, pull out the tent and make camp for us."

"Oh we're not staying the night are we?"

"Better find some driftwood for a fire too." Says the fisherman over his shoulder.

"We can't stay the night!" But Slim is too far away to hear him. Dave absent mindedly reaches to the tire for the beer. It's not there. "What am I doing, I don't drink that stuff." He looks at the cooler. "I know it was on the tire. Looking west towards the sea shore, there are the clammier's bare foot prints with a tipped over cervesa can and the dog licking on it. Joey took it off of the tire and after a swallow said "yuck!" and threw it down. The dog was right behind for beggar's pickings. "Joey you drink water. These other beverages are bad for you, too much sugar." "When Marina talks you listen and do." Even the dog knows this.

In less than two hours the old angler caught four thy length flat fish and Marina dug up around a dozen white clams, no prized chocolate mollusks this time. They all meet up and saunter back to camp. Dave has an arm load of twisted mangrove driftwood. There's something about mangrove wood and flies and they are buzzing all around Dave. He is having a fit and says to Slim "Don't the flies bother you how can you stand them?" Slim purposely steps into a pile of kelp rotting in the sun and of course he is bare foot, sending up a huge swarming cloud of the pesty biting insects all over all of them. The sun soaked Baja surfer looks at Dave and says, "What flies?" Joey laughs and to himself Slim swears he heard is brother's laugh. Dave gasps and swallows six or so flies. He coughs and gags.

"Have another beer Dave." Slim checks the wine bottle in the cooler, opens two ice chest cold tecates, and hands one over to Red's son. It does wash down the bugs. "Build a fire Dave, down there so the smoke goes up the draw, away from us. Not far. We don't want Marina to walk too far from the wagon...there, that's good." Slim talks as he foil wraps the cleaned and fillet fish with added seasoning that he keeps in an old pharmacy prescription bottle. After prepping the fish, he takes the remains to the waters edge, throwing the guts to the crabs that had huddled around him like a football team. The dog got the fish heads.

"Your Dad said you were a 'chuckawala' weblow scout." Dave remembered. He hated camp outs. He knew his Dad liked them though. He chuckled to himself and looked for a place to throw the empty cervesa can. "Toss it to the dog, she knows where they go." Sure enough, there was a pile of empties forming around the front driver's side tire conveniently placed so that the old surfer would not miss cleaning up when he left a camp site. The smell of brew was gone from them, and licked dry. "She will do the same to our dishes," gloated Slim.

Marina put on her favorite music, 'Patsy Cline'. Slim and she had a self designed stereo system which consisted of; a spare twelve volt battery connected to a solar panel, with a CD player. During dinner they will listen to 'Elvis'.

"I-fall-to..pieces"

And it's two fingers to sunset. "Why do you say that?" Joey is toying with some bug with a found stick. "What?" she says. "You know, the fingers to sunset", the lad looks out to sea and a gentle warm breeze tosses back a shock of his hair.

"Where I was born, in the islands of the Pacific Rim, we have no watches. We extend our arm and put our hand across the horizon and the ocean to the sun if it fits between the sun and the edge of our planet, it is noon. No shadows is mid-day. East, the sun rises- it is morning and it is measured by fingers." She said as she opened a can of frejoles and put it over the fire. And as she poured rice into a pot of boiling water, she commented to Dave about the fine fire he built, "Joey, reach in the cooler and bring me a can of peaches. One water for you and no beer."

"Oh he knows not to drink that beverage," said Dave, and he looks down the beach where the can had been in the foot prints. "Na," he said to himself.

Soon all was sizzling and the aromas of beach fire and food made the taste of cold peaches in the can that was passed around to each person hit the spot. It was sunset as far in any direction; north, south, east, and west. The sky was a pale pink as the last blue of the day faded to dusk just before dark.

Their bellies were full, the dog had licked the plates clean, and Marina and Joey were wading in the sea tide washing the dog saliva off with saltwater and wet sand. Slim was setting up the three man dome tent and filling up the queen size air mattress on the floor inside the sleeping quarters. Dave was settled in a low-boy chair with his knee caps up and his bare feet in the still warm sand. He is daydreaming about Red, vaguely, when suddenly he sits up and says "Hey where do we sleep?"

"Oh, I thought you were dosing over there." 'Well a bless my soul- what's a wrong with me- my heart is a itch en like a fuzzy tree, I'm all shook up...' is playing on the CD in the background. "Joey, I made a bed for you in the surf wagon." They have returned from the dish washing adventure and his feet are wet and sandy. Slim laid out a mat of woven palm leaves which carpets most of the padded floor behind 'Ole Gnarleys' space behind the front seats. Two Mexican blankets, one folded for a pillow and the other for a body cover, are laid out over the tatami.

"Can we tell camp fire stories Uncle Slim?"

"For as long as it takes for your feet to dry," says Marina.

It is dark now. "Well Dave you have three options for sleeping tonight," the unshaven boney old man gives one of his mischievous grins. "We that is Marina and I have a three person tent, but I can't figure out; do you want to be next to me, that puts me in the middle, or, do you want to sleep next to the Tongan woman that puts her in the middle. Before you answer, we need to tell you, we sleep naked. There is one more option, you can sleep here next to the fire, on a banana-chair." A banana-chair is a contraption that can fold in many shapes including flat with a length of six feet. Dave makes the logical choice

"Who starts the stories?" asks Joey, "do we all get to tell one?"

"Dave tell us one about your Dad."

"No, I pass."

"Let me start with one about your great grand father Joey."

"Did he surf too?"

"Oh yes indeed."

"They knew about waves then?"

"Oh yes indeed, and they stood up on large planks of shaped red wood. However, great grand father and his friends made a craft that was hollow in their high school wood shop." It was the summer of 1940. 'Fudge', your great grand father was also called 'Fudge' but for different reasons, and his two surf friends had surfed 'dawn patrol' and wanted to get his Dad's 1938 Hudson Terra plane Woodie back to the driveway before he finds out they "borrowed" it. They loose the ignition key. Bill, they call him 'Skiis' because of his abnormally large feet, decides he knows how to bypass the key and start the wagon. He uses a coat hanger that is used to hang up a business suit coat belonging to the Hudson's owner for wire. The battery compartment sits under the wooden floor below the front seat. Smart!, connect it from the battery to the starter. It works! But "Skiis', being ever in a hurry, forgets to take the uninsulated straitened coat hanger off. 'Fudge' put the vehicle in gear, it's one of the first electronic push button transmissions, no shifter lever but it did have a clutch peddle. They get about five miles when they smell smoke. Soon the front floor boards get hot. They stop but don't turn off the engine for fear that it won't start again. They get out and look under the Terra plane and the firewall is on fire. 'Fudge' exclaimed to his friends, "I'm done for by my old man!" Frank, known as 'kick bite and chew', suggests "let's drive it to Palos Verdes and dump it over the cliff at the cove and say it was stolen from your dad's driveway. He can claim it for insurance. 'Skiis' says "Yeah, and we can take the bus home." It takes approximately forty minutes to reach a spot on the cliffs to dump the Woodie wagon and during the way, they each take turns peeing on the flames that are now licking their way into the cab. 'Ole Kick-Bite' would later become a fireman. He got his alias as a high school football player in leather helmets, that was his battle cry- "kick, bite, and chew!". He later taught me how to fish. Any ways, to the story; It was rural in PV then, only a few houses and they picked a desolate field and waited for dark in a ravine. The flames were in the seats and then the roof by then and heading for the gas tank. The young surfers pushed it over with the engine running and the transmission in gear. The 1938 Hudson Tera plane Woodie free fell about twenty feet with the roof and surf boards flaming. It landed grille first and then wheels up on the beach cobbles below. The wreck made lot of smoke which made them nervous, but as the tide came in, the fire went out. There was an article in the news paper and the carcass remained there until it rusted away many years later.

Joe's turn was planned next but he falls asleep and Marina carries him gently to his cubbie in 'Ole Baja Gnarley'. Before she covers him, she washes his feet with bottled water and with her corpulent hands, she gently rubs his legs to his toes with alovera oil mixed with her mixture of plumeria flower peddles from her yard. A tear from each eye falls.

She brings the bottle of pinot grigio and with the pop of the cork a chorus of coyotes howl along the arroyo leading from the desert badlands to the beach at 'bone-yards'. They pass the bottle around and Dave takes a reluctant but long swallow, "Tell me how he died Uncle."

"There's not much to say Nephew..."

Two eyes have been watching the camp since the aroma of food wafted from the fire. And now there are a total of eight yellow orbs peering from the dark shadows. The dog knows they are there, and growls low and now Marina and the man of the desert know they are not alone. They both know it is better not to tell Dave.

"Is all the food and scraps put away?"

"Yes, me and the dog took care of it. I'm ready for sleep." And they crawl into the tent.

Dave is alone, and after click-clicking open the banana chair, he lays on the neatly folded Mexican blanket. He is on his back and closed his eyes, and it came to him- "I'm alone here! At this moment, I am the only one awake. The only one aware. A human, a man, am I in charge? For miles, hours from any one else and he opens his eyes. The moon has not yet risen and so there are no shadows. In just six feet, the length of a man, the darkness has possession of the night. The man closes his eyes again and there again is a chorus of coyotes. "Too much wine." He opens his eyes again and sees stars. For the first time he sees them as a sphere surrounding the earth. A sphere-like mist surrounding the planet. A cloud stretching in all directions to eternity. "I have no control of anything out here!" He closes his eyes once more to sleep and if the man is inclined, to dream.

"Marina, we didn't hear your camp fire story." Slim is up close to her.

"I will tell a good one when the boy is awake." The islander is looking at the sand. She is looking through the fabric of the tent netting as if it had disappeared. She can see neither, it is dark. She sees the sand with her mind. It is the sand of her faraway pacific island beach.

"I talk too much, next time you be first."

"The wine talks too much." She drifts off to sleep.

The wild canines are at it again. This time they are yipping and jumping around themselves. Slim hears them and is trying to determine how many. The furry demons are moving to different clearings in the harsh desert brush and cactus east and above camp. "No one is in charge, must be a mixed pack of both males and bitches." He reckons to the dog. There are in fact two males and two females. All four want personal control. The females have an advantage, they are in unison with their ultimate goal, that being, each will persuade with their promise of procreation. After much growling, jumping in circles, and whining, it is agreed that one of the males needs to take out the camp dog. The bitches agree that they cannot do it because, being a human's dog, it may or may not be castrated and so they could not be certain about the outcome of their sexual desires. The alpha male wants the younger one to do it to show how macho and mature he is and says with body language, "If I go in there, you will probably run off with the girls." The girlies wimper a giggle with each other and circle each other a few times, each with their noses in each other's behind, sniffing for menstrual. The scrawny beasts have convened for too long and now the moon is casting it's influence on the situation by creating shadows in the dim silvery light. The sea sends a breath of breeze with a strong sent of primordial brine as the tide begins to come in.

"Arr!, now I have the advantage." The old salt whistles for the dog and it gladly snuggles in a corner away from the tent flap. They have done this before. The macho male coyote is quite guapo and his young strut does not go unnoticed by the bitches. And not missed by the alpha male. The attacker stealths through the last of the shadows and, at close range for his attack, he realizes that what he thought was a sleeping camp dog was actually a bag of cans and an empty bottle of wine. A gray desert pack rat had gotten it's head stuck in the neck of the bottle. After a few seconds of entrapment, and a few whiffs of wine alcohol, it pulls itself free. It lost it's balance which sent the fur ball and bottle in opposite directions across the undulated bag of debris. The action startled the coyote and he jumped back in a skitter, into the lunar light between the smoldering camp fire and Dave who was dreaming vividly about his wife so far away. The coyote flipped his tail as he tried to look cool and he froze in the sceptically piercing eyes of the other male. He flipped his behind fly swatter again to break the spell and it brushes against the outdoor sleeper's bare shin bone. This woke up Dave in his usual skeptical self, and found he was looking into the yellow devious psychedelic eyes of a large wild canine killer of the baja dessert, not more than a muzzle of teeth away from his nose.

"Do something!" the females yip in unison. And the alpha male did. All three came down quickly with their most ferocious growl baring their teeth. The bitches stopped just before the soft sand of the camp and the male trotted low for the hapless human on the cot, thinking he would go for the throat first thing with his large canines. But before he could get there, Dave screamed and flailed his arms wildly and one appendage struck the first coyote on his dry old leathery feeling snout. It jumped back over the low smoking coals and landed in front of the three-man tent, right in the arms of Slim who had stepped out at that moment, standing strait and naked.

The sorrowful looking surfer was howling as loud as if he had ridden for the first time through the 'three points' surf break. The young guapo coyote leaped off the old man's thin arms and took off like a blue bellied lizard, up the arroyo used as the camp banyo. By now, the other male was within a leap at either man, sensing the moment and not looking at the females, he bars his teeth and growls out a challenge. Dave is froze in his chair, surely because of the hypnotic amber eyes and, just as true for the coyotes, for they all know nothing good comes from looking into blue eyes. It is the scrawny baja man's chance to seize the moment and he runs at the coyote, howling, whooping, just like them. He reaches down to an all fours stance bounding around this time like a jaguar and at the last second he veers off to the left and grips the front fender of the wagoneer and begins humping at the tire with his naked body. Looking at the male wild canine, he yips and yips and humps harder. Some how this aroused the old man's baby maker to erection and upon realizing this, he turns from the fender and walks with his hands on his hips towards the two females. He wiggles his white bleached eyebrows and grins like only this man can do. In the next moment, the two vixens look at each other, then at the unclothed aroused human. Their ears go up and their piercing wide eyes glow red. The alpha male accesses the situation and leaps between the erotic drama quicker than most mens eyes. Then he also hop trots up the arroyo with the two bitches following close to his dewclaws, back into the darkness, to a wild not tamed but by a few sorcerers.

Dave sat there on his banana chair looking subconsciously for light and finally relaxed looking at the camp fire pit. That mischievous gray fat desert rat with a long tail, different, with a paddle on the tip of his whip was seen by the still recuperating man. The rodent appeared to be dancing in the red pulsating glow given off from the twisted burning embers. A low spark explodes and four embers float up about three feet above the coals, cooling in the night air that is moving with the rhythm of the gentle breeze from the night's moon. The rhythms die down and so do Dave's thoughts. He lays down, closes his eyes from the night, and his mind is gone from the world before the coals of the fire have cooled.

There was faint murmurings from the tent and Joey slept through it all. Marina wakes from her dreams of a lover; a young man among men of large sizes, a naive father, a king of his island newly appointed. And of a young boy now ten years old. And she dreams of the sun becoming full over the watery horizon to the east. With a low voice, the sound not much different from the murmur of slow rolling cobble stones in a gentle surf, she says to the old baja hero, "You geeve um? You take care of the night?" as he gently caresses her large moo mooed behind, she realizes his manly protuberance. 'Umm, ah-oh! At your age?" it is their first time.

Joey was first up. "Hey, what happened to the tent? Who let the air out of the mattress?" Dave knew. Just before sun up, the 'pop' woke him up, so suddenly that he lost all recollection of the dreams created in the night. Nothing more was said about the incident, other than from Marina when she and Slim found the opening between the downed tent poles and climbed out with the dog jumping over their backs. They were still naked and, arm in arm, they walked as if on a cloud, sandy and cool from the nocturnal dew, to the sea for a swim. She said, "Must have been a chubasco wind last night."

"Don't look Joey!"

"Does Marina have any chocolate milk?"

"Joey don't think like that."

He wasn't. He shuts the lid of the ice chest and uncorks a fart.

"Joey don't do that. You know where the toilet paper is."

"I didn't do it, the dog did."

"Now Joey, what did your mother tell you about lieing?"

"I'm not lieing, Uncle Slim says 'the dog did it' is how surfers say "excuse me".

"Slim?!" They reach the water and and the white haired old surfer puts his long sinuey tanned arm around her ample waist. "No more coconut milk for you." They dive under the waves.

CHAPTER 3

Nate Oliver Alias 'Tex Ludie'

He is Nate Oliver. "Oliver is not his legal last name for reasons which will later manifest itself. The surfers call him 'Tex Ludie'.

The self generated luminosity of artificial man made light, gave the sonic and echo screen an eerie green color to the echo screen waves and bar code lines which are back dropped in black. Sonics Specialist 2nd class 'Oliver' is involved with his headset, sometimes giving verbal responses to the blips and bleeps he is hearing. He is assigned to the USS- "Blue Fin" on a two year assignment to survey the Mariana trench.

He is from Galveston, Texas which is where he learned to surf, or, where King Neptune took an interest in his skills. 'Tex' took an interest in long wave riding while surfing the wakes of cargo ships off his home shore.

His family is well into the 10% wealthy and quite involved in influential politics. They were not impressed with his choice to join the Navy. 'Nate' personally paid off a lawyer to keep a judge quiet and not inform his family about his "bust" with the law. In exchange, Nate was to leave town. His stature and intelligence made him perfectly suitable for submarines.

Old habits and exotic ports kept 'Tex Ludie' astray but he was able to maintain himself aboard the 'Blue Fin' during the long runs under the sea. The tight quarters and regimented movements were not too much different than a penitentiary cell. The most positive difference, he was doing honorable work.

King Neptune would say he began to unravel when the tattooing started. 'Daga' would say it was a beginning of his animal nature on Earth.

24

Nate said, "The cuts reminded him of his family, a pain." 'Tex' says "I'm collecting art."

Perhaps the long hours in front of the sonic screen played a part also, because all the tattoos are green. In fifteen years from the first cut, his whole body would later take on the color of a frog. He, being with a physique that is a bit corpulent, his over all look would later give the Surfer an amphibious look.

Nate was feeling the scratch-burn of his eighth tattoo session. His short muscular thighs were now scared with ink pricks in West Pacific Rim symbols making the over all look as if he had on a pair of Bermuda shorts. The artistic shorts were covered by Navy issue white boxer scivies which were covered by Navy issue long white pants. He was sitting at his post and his legs were burning like fire. The sub has been out of harbor for ten days and is now a mile deep in the Pacific Ocean's Grand Canyon. The sonics specialist has been at his shift for three hours. Before his shift he was informed, as well as everyone on board by the 'Blue Fin's' Commander, that the USS 'Thresher' was missing. It is 3am somewhere. Somewhere, where the sun shines. Down here, in the wet, high pressure darkness, it always feels like 3am. Tex says his 'smoke' takes away that jet-lag feeling. He never brought 'enhancements' on board.

"What do you mean 'missing' sir?", someone called out.

"Attention men!" Officer Sneed barked out, "there has been no contact with the 'Thresher' in six hours".

"You all will be informed as intelligence is received." Continued Commander Thortch. "Now back to duty."

The 'Thresher' was in the same class of sub as the 'Blue Fin', there were three in this group, all built to withstand deep sea pressure. All three were in rotation for this mission. The missing sub had been in for repairs when Nate's boat arrived. The hydraulics controlling ballast had been replaced and all ships in the three boat fleet were to be checked.

"I hope Kelly is OK," thought Nate. They were to receive dolphin tattoos on their shoulders in Hawaii around a year before. They were following a tradition going back to the 18th century whalers, who said that the symbols will keep a sailer from drowning. It was their last deployment together. Tex reaches to his back, the hair is standing up around the exotic fish tattoos making him scratch at an itch. They ran out of time at the tattoo parlor and Kelly only got one 'Daga' symbol needle-pierced into his left shoulder. He said he would get the other the next time the two sea men were together. There was a metallic grown throughout the sub as it pressurized itself.

Specialist Oliver likes loneness. He calls it solitude.

Nate likes the solitude of the open ocean, weather it be day or night. The freedom of being so far from his family brings loneliness to his heart.

Tex Ludie never felt so alone when he saw the destruction of the Arabian Golf and it's waters caused by the oil greed. "Am I the only one who sees this?"

"It sure ain't purple hays," was Kelly's reply. It was to be the last time they would be together.

Part of the submariner's tradition was to play chicken with Russian subs and the sonics specialists had a distinct role in the game. These guys all had better than excellent hearing, and this test brought out the superior decibel intellect. The game went like this- Which country spotted the sounds first would trail after the other until found out. Officer Specialist Oliver proved exceptional and his sub followed for an hour before being discovered at which time the Soviet sub did a u-turn and faced the 'Blue fin'. The next phase of the game-wars is to close the gap between one another as quickly as possible, keeping record of the time. It was impossible, in the headset noise of bubbles, to tell who flinched first. The noise of bubbles when it came to surfacing a sub was different from when a sub passed by under water. Different subs have different sounds too.

It is a magnificent sight to see a sub in the 'Victory' class break the barrier of air between the sea and sky, known as surfacing, breaking fin, or, becoming visual to mankind's eyes. With telescope or sonar, day or night with human eyes and ears, it was awesome. But not like the experience with whales. Nate has experienced all of the before mentioned, and above all, he's surfed with the swimming mammals of the sea. He would tell you the most splendid of times is when he is with Daga.

There is a saying among Surfers- "Scared right out of the water." This also applies to submariners. This drama was to end Officer Specialist Nate

Oliver's navy career and send 'Tex Ludie' on a wandering Surfer's journey to where he is now.

Nate was on his watch, his six hour shift was in it's fourth hour. The time being 3:05 on a 24 hour time. The 'Blue Fin' had been at sea 16 days of a 30 day sortie. Fourteen of those days were spent a mile below the level of human habitation. At three in the morning it is eerie to most people. A submariner gets used to the strange jet lagged feeling of this time of day. This sensation is a constant on a Navy sub.

A series of blips come to Nate's ears. They weren't faint. They came into the sonics headphones to Specialist Oliver instantly. Not loud or ear piercing, but distinctly comfortably toned. Officer Oliver efficiently text up the computer monitor built into his tight quartered station, it being exactly three feet by three feet on three sides with the chair being in the gang way isle. The location is quite elite among other seamen because its in the bridge area. That is, where the periscope is as well as where the Skipper stands and views the world outside of the sub. The eyes of the crew have seen only bleeps of sonar.

"Oh man what is that?" to Tex Ludie the voice sounded like Kelly. Nate turned to his right and then to his left, but forgot about it as he became intrigued with what appeared on the sonar screen. He instantly electronically signaled the bridge while adjusting the imaging monitor to take up the huge size of the sonic image.

Second Mate Smithe took two choreographed steps and stuck out his tattooed forearm on a bulkhead pipe for balance. Nothing is said. This is strict protocol when the 'Blue fin' and all subs encountered something that is not verified. Instantly the image changed shape, becoming more vertically oval as the sides got thinner. It moved foreword in front of the sub causing a turbulence to the sub, forcing it into an inverted downward spiral, waking the Caption.

"As you were, stand your stations men." It took the Commander three minutes to get to the bridge. Slow, but he had to maneuver while the submersible righted itself. "Two degrees port, ahead five knots. What have we here?" Captain Thortch is from the North Pacific coast. His forefathers being Russian fur trappers and whalers.

The official report of the incident will read; Contact with vessel, 3:05, pursuing at five knots, depth one thousand feet.

"Set depth fins at ten degrees rise, level out at five hundred feet." "What is it? what is your sonics saying Nate?"

"I never heard anything like it sir. It's a rather melodic sound."

"You been smoking that 'wacky tobaccie'? What do you mean melodic." That was the 2nd Lieutenant Smithe.

Nate extended his tattooed hand, looking like a crab with its boney legs being engraved in green ink along the tops of the man's fingers ending just before the finger nail in a dragon-like claw. His index finger pushed a button next to the Captain's arm pit. He jumps back slightly at the hand and begins reading the stats the button brought up, defining the object now moving faster, away from the 'Blue-fin'. It read, "Unknown."

The Captain categorized his military maneuvers in his head in terms of hunting sea animals. "I suspect a whale gentlemen. Readjust speed to ten knots, evaluate speed to close distance to prey. Keep distance of three hundred yards."

"Sir, I have never seen a whale of this size," says Nate.

"Make ready the underwater viewer if you please, Lieutenant." Captain Thortch never regards Lieutenant Smithe by his name which irritates the young officer.

"Maybe it's the purple people eater. What do you think Specialist Oliver?" Smithe is trying to ease the tension at Nate's expense. He knew of Nate's use of psychedelics. He also knew Nate would one day be promoted to Lieutenant and he could not bear the thought of someone not in his right mind running a crew.

Suddenly the object on the screen did an abrupt ninety degree turn to the left and then to the right while still heading strait. On the sonar it appeared to hop from side to side. Right to center, left to center. The sonics in the pilot house became rhythmic, sounding like the beat of a mambo dance.

"Turn off the sub crew sound if you will, Specialist," the Captain calmly said.

Click-click... click-click... click...click...click went the six toggle switches it took to mute the sub.

"Mambo-mambo mam-Bo!" Tex Ludie heard Kelly again in the atmosphere.

"Change course, adjust pectorals four degrees, release ballast, rise thirty feet and level, maintain speed. Let's bring it to the surface," ordered the Captain.

"Sir, the UFO has instantly changed course and is heading directly towards us."

"Yes I can see," said the Captain while looking at the sound sensor.

"Sir, the viewer is ready."

"Let's see what this is," replied the Skipper.

Captains are always fearless as well as cool under pressure. This one is no different. However, this one's hair went up noticeably on the the back of his neck. "Dive! Dive, 45 degree pecks, all ahead full. Level at four hundred feet." This class of sub was built to stay submerged at this depth for an unlimited amount of time.

It happened that the object took offense to the act of the 'Blue fin' trying to get below it. Taking this maneuver as an act of aggression, it suddenly turned and proceeded to confront the sub. Now the 'Blue fin' was heading down uncontrollably.

"Sir!" Now both tattooed hands were violently tapping flashing lights on the sonar board. "It appears that the UFO is circling us." Indeed it was, three times in fact, quickly. It's wake making navigating the man made behemoth impossible. The motion made the ocean into a vortex that sent the "Blue fin' to a depth of over 1000 feet.

"Do not call this a UFO. That's an order!" the Captain now showing his body to be visibly shaken. "Turn off the visual."

"What did you see Sir?" asked Lieutenant Smithe.

"Prepare to surface. It will be in my report."

But the sub was not responding to rising mechanical instruction and was sinking deeper. Deeper than any Victory Class submersible had ever gone. Deeper than the Captain had ever gone. As the pressure gages began to show dangerous readings, the Captain ordered a mechanic to the bridge to fix a leak. It seams a pipe had sent a squirt of fluid onto the right leg of the skipper's white pants around the zipper. Mechanics Mate McDowell turned a wrench around the location of the Commander's crouch even though no leak was visible, accommodating the superior officer's wishes.

Then, leaks were starting due to the depth.

"Sir, the pectorals are warping and will not respond!"

"Yeah, that's what happened to us!" It was Kelly's voice, this time in Nate's earphones.

Nate sent out a distress signal and then in an involuntary move, he gave another distress signal in Morse code with the beat of the mambo. "Good one," was echoed from Kelly. "Sir, the USO has circled under us."

"What is a USO?" said the Lieutenant.

"An unidentified swimming objects are to be reported, swimming or not." Said the Captain

Just then a great rush of sea current seemingly from the ocean bottom, it flowing to the surface, sent the sub sideways to the surface and was seen by a search helicopter looking for Kelly's sub. Now officially missing and never to be found.

There was a formal Navy inquiry which lead to a mass cover up. All Navel personnel involved testified that nothing inordinate happened in order to keep their ranks and careers. Except Nate, who refused to go along with the official record. He would be unhonorably discharged from the Navy on a trumped up charge instigated by Lieutenant Smithe.

But that was a long time ago.

EL TARGO DE AVIAN

Nate became a buffer zone in obscurity. He became known as 'Tex' most of the time and resided in the Baja as a Surfer and renowned bird watcher. His superior hearing made him highly sought after as a partner on birding expeditions.

A knowledgeable birder always brought a person on a hunt who is a target for birds. Birds defecate on such Souls. Perhaps they do it out of fright and they are playing a game of 'how close to a human can you fly'. Perhaps the act is performed out of spite and loathness for man and his clumsy disregard for the wild. Most Souls don't even know it's going on. A random splotch on the shoulder, how inconvenient.

Tex Ludie knows the game, and sea gulls are the most notorious players.

The 'Poser' knows the game. That is why he prefers to have Tex along with him when he is on a birding expedition.

Slim knows also. Tex Ludie will take any beach new comers on a walk along the shore to see how the person will 'measure up' to the sea gulls.

Ludie once got a mouthful. "Don't be looking up," Slim told him. Slim walked with a wide distance from a certain area along the tide line. The turtle leather skinned one had observed that the shore pound waves come rhythmically down the point. The sea gulls observed it and they finished their glide with a fresh dump in this area. The old white haired Surfer never told Tex Ludie about this.

Nate was once bombed by a Snowy White Egret. 'Dapper' was there. They were in the Yucatan. There were many near misses from rare birds that made entry into the two birder's identifiers books. The most prized were a Spoon Billed Ibis, a Turquoise Bro-wed Motonot, and a Masked Tityra.

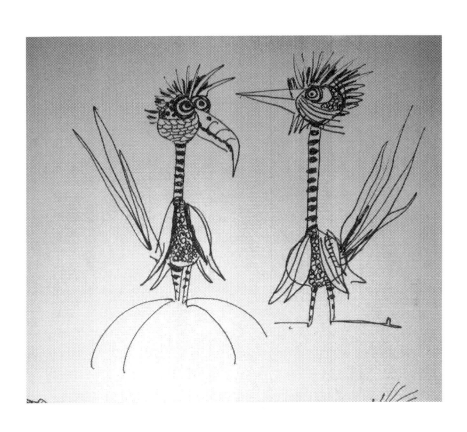

CHAPTER 4

'Dapper' alias 'The Poser'

The humidity though cool still from the desert night, permeated the beach below the bluff. Misty, the color of champaign, with the smell of primordial brine, it filled his lungs for the old surfer as he went through his morning workout. At his age, the exercise was for keeping what muscles and tendons he had left flexible but tighter than supple. It was a movement into positions needed for different stances, poses needed to hold the surfboard edges as they knifed into the faces of waves.

He glances for the first glow of orange sun rise.

The moves were invented by him with a combination of yoga-ti-chi bordering between Asada-strength and Parana- breath. On mornings like this, after strong swells, the energy derived from the atmosphere was, well, intoxicating.

'The Poser', as the surf world knew him, was satisfied with his performance in the surf the day before. As he faced East and inhaled, he closed his eyes and adjusted his regal stance and let the glowing orbs of planetary central fire, the Earth's heat and life, filter through his closed eye lids tuning his mind a deep crimson and the sun's energy permeated through his blood in swirls.

"Thank you Cosmic Creator" he said in his mind.

And so it went as he changed poses in the four directions of the compass never forgetting to cling to the Earth with his toes and with his Soul.

As he awakens from his trans like motions and opens his eyes, he takes in the dawns vision of the carnage rot by hurricane Ned. Over 20 pongas and luxury fishing boats are strewn across the first cove beach. The fillet house has no palm roof and only 3 perimeter palm poles are standing. The slaughter benches are no where to be found. Two 30 foot sport fisher's yachts are on their side against drift wood mooring logs, cracks in the hulls are clearly visible.

Azul turned away his sight from 'Dapper'. The man, (yes The Poser has two interchangeable aliases), rotated his head in the direction of the cliffs. Dapper recognizes his 'grommet' above and they both look away, towards the cemetery on the bluff south-east of town. Azul is disappointed with his behavior the day before. He did not paddle out. Now he is embarrassed to face his mentor 'Dapper'. He is not sure if he should surf in the festivities of this day's 'Surf-in'.

Dapper slept like a driftwood log in May during the Hurricane Ned's stormy night before. His house, made of specially mixed pulverized volcanic pumice mined by the locals and pickup trucked to town and made into cinder blocks from a pit found only at this spot in the Baja. Stone embellished most of Dapper's artistic architecture. It weathered the storm as well as all the homes built with their cinder block mix. The foundation was carved into a Mexican surveyed lot 20' above the town's storm deluge creek bed. The house faced East and was split level. The cobble road, 1-1/2 cars wide, was on the West side, carved into the sandstone cliff, in the sand dunes. The bluff blocked the wind coming from the North and South across a vast plain of desert. The kitchen and bedrooms and bath were on this road level.

The upper level was an open Ramada, it's structure poles were of 2foot diameter palm trunks jackhammer buried into the limestone sub strata of compacted poras coral. It has a three sided deck that wraps around the 20foot by 30foot Baja style cottage with a view of the waves through first and second point as well as the ponga launch beach. The breeze off the ocean was a constant and kept the living area cool, and the flying bugs away. He slept well because he built a four sided 6foot by 8foot cinder block room under the house making the structure almost three stories. The storm and the personal energy he had to expound to surf dance with it, as well as his age, definitely contributed to his slumber.

He dreamed of the pterasaur again. And now, as a flock of pelicans flew by, he remembered the primitive saur's last statement, "why do the male pelicans have red lips on their bills?" Dapper shakes his head to himself and answers, pterodactyls don't talk!?..

He heads his pace towards the trail carved into the cliff from beach to town. "I think I'll wear my aqua-flowered trunks with the black background today. The tide will be best around 11:00." The swell from the tropical storm was still a constant 4' to 6'. He laughs to himself, "good for posing".

Azul is nowhere in sight, but he can see Dapper. He likes to call him Dapper. He can see the village. Do they know his cowardliness? And he sees the olas this morning. They are dark, the color of jade luminous jewels. They are transparent, from the blues of the ceruleans to almost ebony. This was at daybreak, the young Latino surfer knows- "when the olas show the color of fresh spewed volcanic emerald the fiesta will start. But how can he participate? This was for the Hombres. To take the next day left over olas as one would frijoles.. What would they think?

"You bring your family's pico seasoned carne asada and coals of mesquite to the Barbie, you will be welcome". Dapper was thinking fast. He and Azul met in the ravine just after the cemetery.

"Lord, Man, I already miss Red."

The Poser took the old coyote trail through the small dusty town to his dwelling. It started at the cemetery, or, it started one block below the cobble road above La Casa Del Poser depending on which direction a person was going or coming. Confusing? The surfers call this banter cross current talk. "It's two degrees south in an east-west direction. And from there to infinity in either direction". The locals say the trail winds over the Gigantor mountains to a small town on the Sea of Cortez. "40 miles towards the morning sun."

Red always bought fresh carne from a rancho South, up the canyon from town, where he and 'Tex Ludie' had their oasis. Azul's family also had a rancho up the main river north of the small coastal village. "Come over to mi casa Azul I have a special camisa for you to have." Dapper uses his charm and soon has the teen light stepping along the trail to 'La Casa Del Poser'. The trail is old. Older than the town. It is older than before any humans saw the territory. It is well respected. When the Federal government came and put the lots, officially served, in a grid pattern for civic maps, and when fences were put up between lots, the people, the new residences, put gates along where the trail meets a man made barrier. The newest members of the barrio, the people of European decent, had the most problem with the fence. The meandering dirt path is earthy, animalistic, primordial, in this, the Baja, it is much more in charge of things than the will of humans. Ah the stubborn ones, they would die or have the planet die if that is to be the outcome of two wills. For the Poser and Tex Ludie, and Slim, to go with the flow is a surfer's greatest achievement. It was Red who taught this.

It was the Poser who went to town upon finding Red's body slumped and rolled into the sand looking not much more than a clump of sea weed.

He was driving alone. The swishing of wet sand along the deeply ribbed tires of Slim's Jeep Wagoneer was all that could be heard. There was the eternal hum, the low roar of small surf. And then there was a flock of noisy jabbering squawking laughing sea gulls flying along both sides and front of the vehicle's windows. This brought Dapper back to the shore, back, away from his thoughts. Thoughts about age, the man and his surf friends would finally have to face, have to 'deal' with- the end. "Fortunate Red, he will not have to surmise what it will be like when one of us is gone." Dapper was thinking to himself.

'Zeta', Slim introduced her to Joey as "Auntie Zeta" in a Southern antibellem ascent. She took the news hardest, and would not go to Red's wake. She let the tears flow quietly as she filled the ice chest in the back of Ole Gnarley. "I'll make sure ice will be sent out every day until you guys return," she closed the door on the outdoor ice machine. She refilled all eight of her 14x18 inch plastic tubs with purified water filtered in town from the now shallow creek that flows year round just north of the village. She is the the ice maker of town. She lives in a 12 foot travel trailer surrounded by an oasis of palm trees and flowers and vegetables. She's been here since the 70's hippie days. This landscape in the desert is all her creation and is always 10 degrees cooler than any where else around. In the old days she would gather the rare exotic native plants and get them to grow around her 3 lots that her 1st husband, a Mexican National of prominence, bought her. Her gathering instincts gave her the Baja name 'Zeta', (Ant). In the shade from the harsh sun, in her created shadows, she survives and only comes out of her driftwood gate at evening, just before dark to walk her dog returning just after dark. The native people consider her a bruja.

It was Red who visited her regularly after her 2nd alcoholic husband died unexpectedly. It was Red who took her to the airport for a plane to Guadalajara so she could tend to her 1st husband until he died of brain cancer and Red escorted her home. Home to her beloved oasis, which in her absence was taken care of by the legendary surfer.

She is 70 now. The Baja sun has wrinkled and permanently darkened her skin making her very susceptible to cancers.

Zeta and Red go back in their experiences of the Baja from the 60's. A time before highway 1 was complete. They would reminisce for hours... of a time, during which they would consume quarts of pacifica cervesa, dreaming awake of the days, the weeks, sometimes months of living free on deserted beaches on the Baja side by the Sea of Cortez. They would remember to each other of the times of following sport fishing boats on foot. Strolling in the coarse golden sea shell sand barefoot following the marlin flagged boats to the measure and weigh station on the dock at Los Cabos. The sport fisherman were only interested in their trophy picture and maybe a steak sliced from the fillet of the great dead fish. The two would remember together getting 15-20 pounds of meat along with the Mexican Natives.

They would talk until the palm shadows in the oasis were long... the only hotel on the cape being a place for a refrigerated beer and they bring a large dog in who lounged on the cool, adobe tiled floor during the coming of the Full Moon, and it glowed as shimmering silver liquid luminescences across the waters of the Sea Of Cortez.

'Zeta', she devised the Baja hot shower. She let the water, hot from the black 100 gallon tank above her head, flow from gravity upon her naked body under some of her palm trees three hours before sunset. She is definitely feeling alone, tears flowed from her eyes. Tears flowing not much slower or hotter than the outdoor shower head. "I am the last of us. Who will I remember with now?" She shudders, not from being outside naked, but from grief. It was her chihuahua dog whose tail wag breaks her from this spell of self pity. "Good boy" she says, and she smiles seeing in her mind Red putting his right hand fingers to his lips and he then waving goodbye with a kiss. A warm dry Baja wind engulfs her and she is dry before she grabs her warn yellow bleached towel.

"Careless will take ice to Red's resting place tomorrow." She smiles, gazing towards the direction of the surfer's send off. It was a long smile with her beautiful Hollywood eyes, open lipped as if she had a full mouth of movie star teeth. Even with no front dentures she did not cackle. She might have if she had gone to the send off.

"Who will be the last one on the waves? Yeah! Standing, carving that final watery crescent of cosmic energy... Probably Tex Ludie," he chuckles to himself. The old surfer puts his elbow up and rests it onto the Wagoneer's window frame. He adjusts the rpm speed to stay with the flight of the sea birds.

"Tell Marina Red has been found." Tell her; Slim says we will send my brother on his way, his departure from us, where we found him. Bring supplies for three days." "Tell her; let the village know. We will bring his memories back in three days but come celebrate everyone, his departure Saturday night." "Bring 7 llantas." "Bring Red's 8-track music."

A bump and squeak of the four leaf springs under 'Ole Gnarly', as the surf vehicle crosses the shallow ravine with no water; signals he has reached town. He returns to the steering wheel with his mind. "It's getting harder, longer to stand up and surf," the old salt says to himself. His white goatee and handlebar mustache blowing in the wind concealing his moving lips. "I'll wear my black surf shorts with my black and white stripped Russian designed military t-shirt." And as things would have it, so did Tex Ludie.

After a moment of silence, and the tears half found on the perimeter of Marina's eyes had subsided and dried, dried quickly from the noon sun, she petted Dapper on his boney shoulder and said, "I'll be ready five fingers from sundown."

Dapper remembers. He remembered Zeta's eyes as his eyes watered from the coals of mesquite while he tended the barbecue above second point at the Cantina. He was grilling the 40 pounds of carne asada for the town after the hurricane. It is fiesta time.

He watches a fine wave roll through the point beach below him. "Maybe I'll become a 'Sup'. Na, I'll lose respect out in the line up."

"Hey Azul, you stink, you better go surfing and clean up." He could tell Azul likes the new shirt. It was a new beige button down close to the Mexican wedding style but with less flamboyance. It had a print designed by an artist from Mazatlan. It was not hard to notice the young surfer had his mind on waves and not of feeding the town. His work was done, he delivered the meat and mesquite from his rancho. He had endured the ridiculed eyes of his family as he headed to the beach barbecue. "Flojo surfers."

There was a stand up paddle surf rider in the line up along with an assortment of maybe 11 other surfers. "A sup surfer- is he a sub surfer?" the thought passes through The Poser's mind.

Through the grill smoke Dapper watches 'Mr. Magoo', alias 'Rip Curly', paddle standing up, into a wave down the bluff 200 yards from the Cantina. He catches the wave with a modified canoe oar. His stance on the over sized board is different from normal surfing. There is a space between his legs of about 6 inches and his feet face parallel and strait forward. There is a lot of hip movement in the paddling motion. "That would be hard for Slim," The Poser says to himself.

The Poser observed Rip Curly weave his over sized surf rider through the crowd, through the inside of the bay. From the cantina's barbecue pit above, the waves take on a crescent shape. They rhythmically, mechanically, curl along the shore for about the length of 2 football fields. The other surfers in the bay paddle and maneuver around the standing paddle boarder.

"Slap-Fannie!" it is 'Tex' talking into The Poser's ear that is away from the surf.

"What?"

"Here!" Ludie hands a fresh squeezed margarita to the cook. "It's only got 1/2 jigger of tequila."

"Thanks!.. What?"

"I said 'slap-fannie'. That's what I'll play when I can't push up and to stand on my surfboard."

"Slap-Fannie? What's that?"

'Tex Ludie' answers, "It's like counting coup."

"Counting coup?"

"Come on Dap. The native Americans used to do it instead of killing each other. I'm going to do it with a sup-paddle instead of killing these surf Comanche intruders to our surf spot." A large whiff of seasoned asada and mesquite smoke curls around both surf riders.

Tex samples a bite of the asada, "not bad for carnage-carne road kill." He is referring to 'Road Kill Robertos' stew. He is the village butcher. He makes a heavily spiced soup made from the animals killed after hurricanes, cows goats chickens, possums raccoons pit bulls, horses... Slim tolerates it.

CHAPTER 5

A Well Dressed Surfer

Dapper was a shareholder in more than a few of the international surf clothing companies. He invested early in the 1960s and watched his money wisely. His family has been in the New York garment industry for generations. He made most of his profits merchandising sun glasses, but he always kept his wallet in surfer's clothing in order to get the latest fashions for his own use. Now, with the Internet, he is able to spend most of his time here, in this small village with good surf every month for most of the year. He hand selects his own surf wardrobe of course but the guys in town are never without gear.

'Dapper' still gets plenty of promotional goods.

Nothing is ever ordinary in the Poser's life. Take in the color of the ocean he sees. It is noon and as he stands ankle deep in the surf just before the white water foam, below the slope of golden sparkled white sea shell granules of sand, he faces the tide flow and breathes in the briny air. Giving his thanks to the sun rise, he is personally thankful for a slight rest. The walk up to his home will be a workout in itself.

First light beamed sporadically across the tops of Mt. Gigantor. There was a warm haze in the air. It never let the night bring the moon's shade of blue shadows. The sultry haze did not let the sun's shadows show upon the village or beach. When it did let the sun burn through the mist became rolling clouds the color from moon blue to sultry gray and billowing through was white, the hue of Ashien bark and a silver like the ash after a drift wood fire.

The sky is now powdered all colors of white and gray making the atmosphere appear as a huge battlefield of cannon smoke. This makes the sea and the glassy waves appear the color, as Tex Ludie says, 'Nazi Normandy'. He is referring to the gray-green uniforms warn by the German defenders along the French coast during world war two.

The Poser had Juanita Maria, an artist living with a Frenchman in a small beach town a day's journey south, design a fabric cloth for surf trunks this color. Every body in the village got a pair.

This day is especially warlike because even though there is no wind, the clouds appear quite vociferous as a thunder booms like a voice of some entity echoing among the canyons and arroyos across this desert peninsula.

Naturally The Poser is in his token color surf apparel and is holding Tex Ludie's approval. For some reason Ludie is surfing in the buff.

Marina is waiting on the smooth sand between the dry powdered sand and the fresh wet slurry, and to Dapper's delight, she is wearing her 'moo-moo' long dress fitting smartly in the same patterned print cloth with the same pattern of green and grays. There is a chevron of black and gold bands along the sides and bottom hem. Here and there in the background of the gray-green are fist size puffs of Japanese chrysanthemum shapes the color of red orange hazy gray looking like cannon fire across her ample posterior. A design taken from a French painting by Jon Pitre of Napoleon's battle at Waterloo. The ends of the petals fade into a tie dye form of clouds.

"Watch out for the coral chunks!" Tex gives a wave of acknowledgment, Slim gives his smile to everyone as they look around their feet for the shell like objects that are littered about the shore line. Everyone finds a safe path to their sandals. Marina wades out to help Slim.

The patterned cloth did not sell well on the world market. There was also a glitch in the trunk manufacture and a large shipment of 3x size pairs were produced. They didn't go well with the village fishermen either. During the state fishery inspection, they used the trunks to cover the outboard motors during the ponga lineup beach inspection. The inspection Governor stopped for a moment at the neat rows of Government leased equipment and some say they saw his eyebrows go up for a second, above his dark sunglasses. He walked on and said nothing. He did twitch his large black machismo mustache though.

It is the time of year when high noon brings on the 'Baja Bake', Pescadors, surfers, even the lizards find shade. Everyone except of course the mad perros, the Englishmen and Tex Ludie. He has to take a noon day surf ride 'Ala Natural'. The town's Mayer doesn't like it and the church people, well... Red surmised noon was good, everyone knows he will do it, so, they look for shade.

"He better not plunge-splash and swim." Marina and Slim turn their backs to Tex and head towards the fish fillet palapa. "Worms make good bait this time of the year."

"Yeah, red snapper fish. Let's see if there's any on the tables, and caught today."

The shade of the palm frond roofed Ramada at La Casa Del Poser is a welcoming sight but until the sea breeze begins, the deck will be sultry.

High noon, it doesn't take a wrist watch to tell the time as is most of the time in this place. This sphere of geography, this satellite navigated biosphere of our living earth, is a timeless place. This place of the Cosmos is a surfers paradise.

The overcast was warm before the night ended. There had been no moon the night before and the mist of warm took over the twinkling of a million stars. The satellite GPS system belonging to Dapper reported at 1:30 AM 1 million and 3 stars. The computer attached ocean buoy signaled no stars at 3:30, 6' waves, 6 waves in sets at 15 minute intervals.

The sun would shine into a wispy white cloud and turned it to mango-orange and an angry dark gray cloud would close itself against another gray twirling cloud causing a rumble across the sky. The fishermen watched the horizon from the beach along side their pongas and the farmers from a place of safety. The surfers watched the sea too. All were watching for lightning. So far, the clouds brought only thunder and no bolts of electrically charged light. One bolt did come down on the desert about 20 miles south of town killing a flock of pelicans. A short rain squall came minutes after. The lightning makes the fully tattooed man's noon surf ride dangerous.

Now, as high noon approaches, the clouds are thinning, they are parting enough for shadows to appear, and seeing hints of blue around the clouds signal the cooling sea wind will breeze into Dapper's Ramada.

Red would have stayed on the beach and waited for Ludie's wave carve. They all knew it. Especially Nate. Nate knew as he remembered Red, after a shot of round bottle mescal and a cold noontime cervesa, he would 'Discuss the surf performance'. Tex Ludie reminisces about the first apparel-less surf ride.

Now, as the overhead noon shadows tell, Tex Ludie rides again!

The light balmy breeze blows lightly along the sea causing light refracting chatter and making the wave faces to lose their mirror. It is now, at this moment, that neither Tex or Nate can see their image reflected to them from the sea. It is realized, Red will not see this performance. Red will not be on the beach walk today. I will not get my noon ride telecast judged from 'Red'. Who will there be that can give me an unbiased score to the ride based on; wave selection, time of day, water condition, and time alloted for the proper wave. Closer to noon rated best and of coarse originality-style and grace.

Nate came up to Dapper's ramada, as usual, in time for the first cold pitcher of margaritas. He reaches to the solar powered fridge and opens it and fingers a frozen glass cocktail tumbler. Dapper, holding the surf searching binoculars and leaning on the hand shaped and varnish finished rail, calls out in crisp military tone "6".

"Wha?" Nate finishes his pour. A slight smirk comes to his whole being. Tex Ludie sandal slap saunters surf style out to the palapa roofed shady breeze and joining The Poser, he counters with "I got 7 on my first ride." And what about the lariat ride he remembers to himself. He scored highest with Red for that carve.

Using strict military language again, "There will be no props, no ropes, and no lariat slinging. I only judge pure surfing.

"What? You mean no 'Captain Ahab one legged SS style?" the 'Matador' style, he wants me to do the matador style. Ludie smiles and looks out over the sea. They both drift across the oceans sparkle and see the gold of Red. Then, turning, seeing each other's eyes, they smile, a whole being smile like only surfers can do.

The 'Surf Style' is to be left up to each individual Judge. It is not proper etiquette to challenge the Judge. This was an instance this day, and a good chance for Tex to confirm the presence of Dapper as the new official Judge. "There was a 3 second moment while surfing the wave on the fast curling inside, I rode palms out, giving the falling wave lip a two handed low five. I was protecting myself in the lower pubic area, however, not a hair was touched."

"It was noted, as was the 'Statue of David' foot stance." Was Dapper's reply. Tex Ludie was 10 years younger.

"Are we going over to Slim's later for a fish barbecue?" Nate's matter of fact statement surprised Dapper. Nate was in town mostly for the swell and he always stayed at The Poser's place during such times. Both he and Red.. Dapper quickly realized Tex Ludie's surf god was gone.

"Oh yeah, well maybe." Things in town were done when a person wanted to. Besides, Dapper hadn't been feeling well. That is, not like a 100% surfer.

"They're cooking red snapper! I'll get two fillets." Tex Ludie is out the door. He doesn't sit still much.

By after noon, that is, after a cold margarita, Dapper needed a siesta. Yes, it is quite fashionable and almost imperative to do so for his heart. He hasn't said anything here but in his business visits to the United States, he saw the family Physician.

"Well, it's not like you're living in the New Yorker fast lane." Dapper's doctor brings up on his computer images of his patient's latest cat scan. "Dan," says the long time Physician in a sorrowful tone of voice, "the tests show even without the usual business stress that is associated with other family members, I regret to tell you, but you have a heart the equivalent of a 62 year old man."

Even with his laid back Baja attitude, Dapper is feeling rather upstart. In his chest, a line of nerves and internal organs under his calloused surfboard muscles over his sternum and ribcage began to ache. "Doc," he says, "I am 70!"

"It says here," the Doctor is looking at typed past records, "It says here you have a history of imbibing alcoholic beverages. Perhaps if you cut back, you know, maybe even quit the consumption.."

Their eyes meet in the artificial light of the office. The Physician gets a stir in his Soul as if he was looking into the eye of a tiger shark.

"No Azul today," are the thoughts of The Poser as he lounges in one of the hammocks on the ramada. "Is he afraid of the roar in the thunder clouds?"

The Poser dreams into a land far away. A lone continent far away. Away back in time, a place surrounded by water. Huge expanses of turbulent mineralized-saline water. A liquid, tepid cauldron of prehistoric non human life.

He dreams about the Doctor's computer image, and as he focuses deeper into his dream, the liquid image clears to a satellite GPS view of town, but it is changing the view slowly, as if receding in time. The character, as has been lately, is about a Pterdondon. This time the focus is clear that The Poser is witnessing the last Pterdondon of the species. The eye of the dream is lifted as if it was the lens of the GPS. It was showing a harsh and savage land strewn with volcanoes. Another view shows the land splitting a crevice as deep as the Grand Canyon and as long as the Colorado River. There is a peninsula wedged away from a large land mass. The dream shows it's coordinates by satellite. They are from the west side of the Mexican Yucatan to Arizona, United States.

The dream time line moves to the dawn of man. Red men, Shamens, and they are collecting large petrified bones of flight from a strange sea bird.

At a controlled campfire on the beach, a flute is played. It is an instrument made of the petrified flight bones of a large now extinct dinosaur. The music tells the story from the blue rocks surrounding the desert fire. The stones more ancient than the birds. The melody tells of a time long ago. A time of the first pelicans, and the last of a flying dinosaur.

In his dream, Dapper stokes the campfire with Baja desert iron wood and the hot embers entices the flute player to continue. The song is now as vibrant as the flames and the circle around the fire has pelicans with outstretched wings. The flute music sings as a chorus of coyotes howling across a vast desert sand peninsula. A hiss of flame shows as wide as the Grand Canyon. Now it is ocean. The scene is the same. The act of a Pterdondon flying across the chasm. The chasm becoming wider and wider with huge earthquakes.

Now the dream-focus slightly changes to a scene of volcanoes spewing hot molten globs of lava, large fist size, as rain and cooling along the edges of this vast sea.

The flock of pelicans are forced off their roost by a wild fire of brimstones. A Pterdondon's unfeathered leather wings are singed by the flames due to his long takeoff flutter. He organizes the flock into a flying squadron. He taught them to keep the strongest first. The flight is far. Farther than any pelican has flown. Farther than a Pterdondon can go with burnt wings.

The eye of the Pterdondon stared out of the dream, into Dapper's dream eyes and the dinosaur says- "Stay with the flock."

The shadows are long and the last of the sun's rays are reflecting off the church windows when Dapper wakes up. Azul is taping him on his sinewy shoulder.

"An official looking thing from Los Estados Unitos", thinks the young native Baja surfer.

Its from Dapper's family. They want him to come back for more tests. He lays the letter on the hammock and it blows to a corner on the tile floor before he has a chance to ask, "Where have you been? There's Waves! Come on, you like red snapper fish?"

CHAPTER 6

Fire Rhythms I Had No Dance

He remembers. Yes... he remembers the night. Along with many other thoughts in the time when good souls sleep restfully. For him they are past thoughts of dreams played out by himself during his existence. And now they are thoughts of fire. A fire so hot that it melted the Tecate cervesa cans that are placed on a drift wood stick shoved into the drinking hole. The cans were placed in a precise pattern designed by all in attendance and finalized by angles in a concentric circle mentally calculated by Tex Ludie and carried out by him.

His thoughts, "How barbaric. The family was right. I should not stay here."

The cervesa cans line the outside of the 'llanta' bed and above the seven used road tires lays the silhouette of 'Red' rippling in the vortex of heat rising low, before the 450+ degree oval wall of fire. It took all 3 cases of beer cans to complete the funeral lift off design. Ludie had seen the drama once in Indonesia.

It was somehow decided as all ignited the tangled mangrove kindling. One by one, the person who stoked the fire with a can was to do a dance until his beverage container was consumed by the flames.

By far, Tex Ludie was the most gregarious and he handed the fire circle a large quantity of the empty cans. The heat of the fire, as it took hold of the driftwood and tire merger, brought the participants of the 'Wake' back 6' from the rock edges. It was during the time, after the Mexican Pescadors and Azul had finished their cervesas and the conversation mixed with both Spanish and English sentences had run out, that Nate started the dance by taking a mouthful of Round Bottle Mescal and blew fire at the crimson surf trunks still attired by 'Red'.

"Why must I remember this?" He said to himself as he stared into nothingness, reminiscing the last night's moonless night.

Ludie's first round of dance was in his thin soled huaraches. He was using them to detect harmful things attacking his feet. He would squat and hand grab things dangerous and toss them into the fire. He would skip-prance around the fire and stop at each person, offering a swig from the botelo de mescal. I was first! And I handed the alcohol liquid back. We did good, only two containers were consumed. Marina coy fully kept the beverage out of the reach of Azul.

Between the quick can of beer and snort of mescal, and with the pulsating rhythms of the now glowing embers of driftwood, the 6 Mexican Fishermen were mesmerized by Marina's enchanted Pacific island dance of good bye. She hula danced a sway of good bye and the sound of the moo-moo material on her thighs sounded like a sigh. And with a mighty thought pattern she signaled for more wood for the flames. She stomped her large bare feet in rhythm, left to right, and with eyes wide, the brightness of flames began reflecting her gaze causing a gasp from Azul. She raises her arms to shoulder hight and claps the fingers of her large hands to her palms causing a strange tapping sound. She points at Slim and he claps two desert dried sticks together. She points at the sticks and stares into each persons eyes. When all eleven are in unison with found sticks, the flames rise higher than Red had been tall. She clapped the strange sound as she sashayed around the fire until her Tecate can burned to white dust.

"It was I who stoked the fire that time!" he remarked somewhat sadly into the night's darkness.

The large flying embers rose 15 feet, maybe more in the ink black night sky as Slim slammed a large heavy 6 foot log of desert mesquite hardwood next to the now burning red Phil Edwards shaped three stringered surfboard. Red was woven with strands of fresh kelp like Herman Melville's Captain Ahab was wrapped with ropes on the white whale. 12 logs were added to the fire in all. All were large. Larger than the legendary surfer's brother should have carried. With Marina's deep grunt, he switched to the beach sea weed and kelp and it's smokey infernal covered up any profile of Red's cadaver. All the while Ole Slim was in a sort of skip-dance that brought some of the Mexican fishermen to a clap and huff song, very machismo. As the leathery old surfer's can burnt down, Marina was quick to retrieve the teary eyed brother.

"How could I participate in such nonsense? It was I who rolled over more sea kelp." He said to his thoughts. "And Azul.."

As the tires become engulfed in flame, the smoke, thick with the smell of chemicals and synthetic rubber, brought Ludie to another dance with the mescal. He too would stoke the fire, white hot, with more hard desert wood. This time he would hop on one foot, slap his bare tattooed chest with both hands inward, and slap alternately the back of his hand to the upcoming skin-inked thy. Between the very acrid black smoke and the fact that Ludie was in and out of the smoke in translucent nakedness, the attending Pescadors left into the darkness waving and saying in their minds "Adios" to 'Red".

"I never even thought of leaving the Odyssey," echoed in his mind, "How could I?"

It was the planet's high tide that would wash away the night's activities of cremation.

A voice came to the tormented Soul. The voice of the night. As He faded away into the thoughts of dreams, faded, as the ashes of Red dissipated into the sand, wet with the surge of an incoming high tide, this day, just before sunrise, the nocturnal voice said- "You have no dance."

CHAPTER 7

Take Me ON

He says, with a change into proper diction and a bit of a change in the tempo of speech, "I spotted an Amazilia yucatanesis." Nate hands over the binoculars.

"Si!, Si!, es verdad. Esos dos, amigos."

They are not only cabin porch spotters of the avians, they have been around the world. Their favorite location- the Yucatan. They expedition with the International Birders Association, the I.B.A, traveling with world wide members. They like to go together. They do surf and some of their favorite wave carve reefs are lined with forest sanctuaries that are home to long tailed colorful tropical humming birds.

They are planning a trip. Is it their last? The thoughts do come more often now that Red is gone.

For the last two outings they hired a guide. In the Yucatan they imported a vehicle. This alone takes up most of the expenses. A good thing though, four wheel drives make good barter when one leaves. One saves money on the return shipping costs and the burden of looking after it. They didn't sell the last one. It was given as a surprise, (suprido), to someone in the town most charming.

Having lodging close to the best birding forest weighted a long way in the judgment call which had to be accepted by all, with a unanimous verdict by three persons. This means a third person was to be chosen as a voter from the other birders. As an after thought, carried out British rule style, it was decided if a female was chosen for the committee there would be a vote from four birders. Also, it was decided between the two surfers that a couple forming both genders was most acceptable. But what about the other socialites?

The tanned leathery ole salts looked at each other, their eyes glistening in the shade, and smile with teeth as white as coral stained from the minerals of the sea. Tex Ludie pulls the neck down on his collared shirt to relieve some of the tropical heat and reveals the tattoo emblazoned around his neck encircling an inch below his Adam's apple. The tattoo is in a color of green and is seen as a reflection in a mirror in the hotel room. It is of a curling-roping wave.

'The Poser' smiles. The reply taken as a re-verb-echo in Ludie's sharp hearing, "That sound I performed is what I recalled being played by Red on his slide guitar." Vibrating Ludie's brain was Reds rendition of the song 'La Paloma'.

The chill- only for a moment, came over Nate as his mind watched the image of his Navy sonar friend became engulfed in a liquid looking like the deep color of lapis lazuli clear.

It should be noted that their month in the Yucatan was spent only in sanctuaries known to not inhabit jaguars. Their logic-in the sanctuary's, there would be more birds in a habitat devoid of large felines. The paradox is, in the untouched flesh around the inked large turtle tattooed on Tex Ludie's back is the image of jaguar spots. The skin being injected by pure India ink and lines scraped into his epidermal of gold. Two inches above the pelvis, the scene ended with a rope-like sash shaped like the bottom of an English nobleman's vest. The spots wrapped around his torso ending in lapels imprinted with 2 opposing elaborately colored humming birds. The art was done by a well known Portuguese after the surf swells had subsided.

For 10 days, as was predicted by the two after observing the wave and wind action on Dapper's computer, suggested that they would have waves around a certain time in a certain month.

The jaguar spot tattoos were imprinted after the swell to insure a better chance of no infection.

Their chosen guide on that excursion was a local mestizo with a talent for language who's name was Aviano though he liked to be called by his native name. It was hard to pronounce. The guys did their best. He was quite attentive to the diction of English as spoken by these two surfers. The guys thought that their Californio talk would be impressive but it wasn't due to the problems Spanish rule has in this part of the country. Aviano preferred his ancient Mayan dialect.

Their vocal knowledge came in handy for overhearing other conversations from people not realizing the surfers bilingual capabilities.

Aviano convinced the duo to rethink their strategy concerning Jaguars. "Smaller cats, no more smaller birds." He was referring to ocelots and... which also inhabit these new world tropical forests. "Larger cats eat many animalitas."

The surfers gave the guide the name with his permission. They asked him what his Mayan name was. They felt rude by not being able to pronounce it properly. And though they always tried during the duration of the trip, they would laugh at themselves along with their new Central American friend and would again call him Aviano.

The wave riders heard rumors of surf in other sanctuaries known to inhabit jaguars and with the new logic from their guide, a change of plans opened up new possibilities. Spontaneity in the field can cause unforeseen problems. The IBA was a big help in planning locations for the adventure. International surfers of Mexican decent pointed out the good reefs and points on the tropical peninsula in South-Eastern Mexico. British Birders who had been to the Mexican Caribbean e-mailed advice also. Timing and logistics were the challenge. They did find a time slot when a group of Birders did coincide with the coming surf swell.

The haunting dots of the skin imprinted vest were behind the scaled fins of the elaborated image of a turtle. The rear fins extended below and covered his buttocks.

At the end of the Tahiti surf trip with Red, Tex got a tribal tattoo in dark green covering what would be done in the shape of Bermuda shorts. The rear tortuga fins appeared outside the intricate line-symbols circling the man's thys. Tex Ludie's logic being that the sea swimming amphibian's fins need to be free to swim in this atmosphere. It was in these South-West Pacific Rim Islands, that they found with the consumption of a 'cava-cava' concoction that the pain of punctures was reduced. It is rumored that under Ludie's short, braided, dirty-blond colored canonier's tail of hair, is tattooed the back of a loggerhead turtle's cranium. Scaled to the size of Tex's scull.

The turtle shell rings and realistically scaled fins were inked during his de-tension sentences to the Baja prison. The art work started from the neck area, on the back, and down. It was done in shades of green and sea kelp brown, looking very much like a live tortuga. The scaled front flippers extended around the upper arm surf muscles to the elbows.

Red said, "A most exquisite art, and so Earthy," with his eyes glowing and his perfect-man smile.

Red was there when Ludie's front breast plate was hand tapped in. It was to be a likeness of a New Zealand bush lizard. It was agreeable, especially to Tex Ludie who insisted on lizard colors from California.

Red never got there intellectually, but he sure caught on to the value of cyber space. He said, "I may be illiterate to that dimension in the cosmos, but I have found a way socially to overcome this now Earthly inadequacy with a friendly tongue and smile."

It was a wonder time for Red. It was he who found the lizard images on Dapper's computer in 'Captain Nemo's Command Center'.

Yes, Nate will miss the legendary surfer, but before he forgets, he will remember the first day they united. A hurricane was coming. Tex was traveling alone. He set up a camp along side a small cove-like beach with a large bolder resembling a crab that finished a short perfectly sectioning wave. Time wasn't necessary for the mind Ludie was in. He had in his possession a case of fine Spanish wine laced with LSD syringed through the corks. The lone surf rider gathered a large pile of firewood though he knew he needed a small fire only for grilling, the weather was warm, or no flames at all for the night. The astronomers, Nate being one, were preparing for a lunar eclipse on this night. Tex was 200 miles from any man made light. The cloud formations were showing a tropical storm to the south-west, moving north-east, and floating in a direction that will bring waves to this small point on the Sea Of Cortes close to the southern tip of the Baja.

Around sunset or as Slim would say, "It was 2 fingers before sundown and I saw that stack of driftwood and thought maybe I wouldn't have to beach comb."

He and Dapper stepped out of the slightly rusty, in need of paint, Jeep Wagoneer, 100 yards up point from Tex's camp and watched the surf line for a while realizing the 4 inch shore pound was not showing surf-able waves. They conjured up a 2 foot set and followed the 4 waves along the shore to the lone man's camp.

Tex Ludie looks into their eyes and says, "Well now, there will be three riding tomorrow."

"Better make it four, Red's coming. I'm Dapper." He gave a wide eyed smile as Tex looked him over.

"Red?" A smile came over the lone camper as he flipper smacked Dapper's young strong sinuous arm. He stepped back to keep a vantage point between the two recently arrived surf riders.

"We'd like to share some opium tar and mint leaves with you and your fire," Slim said looking at his companion knowing the short, stout, loner's slap would have knocked anyone but a surfer out of balance.

"6," points Ludie. In his mind he too conjures waves.

Just before dark, the waves were up to a blue-green translucent water color hue as Tex fished from shore using spark plugs as weight to the line on his 6 foot surf fishing pole.

Slim had the fire glowing with red hot coals and Dapper had a proper table set for 4 and then Tex came back with 6 sand bass, gutted, along with 4 straight clean, dry driftwood sticks, about 3 feet long.

His timing was impeccable, in a down wind dust, just before the sticks of skewered fish were placed on the fire, up slides to a four wheel slide stop, the Marmon Harrington 47 Buick Road Master Woodie that all Californios know belongs to Red. He Frisbee-throws a warm fog lined bag of flour tortillas to the cook. "Thought we would like these." He steps out of the off-road vehicle, "I waited in town for fresh ones."

"Tex Ludie huh?" Red side steps wide to the left and swiftly grabs hold of Tex's right hand in a grip that could hold on to a waving flipper of a large sea turtle and smiles. "I have a bottle of wine to go with our meal Dapper."

Tex is looking into the eyes of the famous surfer. All four persons around the hot desert fire laugh as all men of the sea do. Red fin-slaps Ludie's left arm. The three new comers to camp are impressed with Tex Ludie's leg balance.

"Late night to 2 hours into early morning, military time; 0100 to 0300," Nate-Tex Ludie quoted to his new friends. It will be a time none of them will want to forget. The stars became a dome of universal planets. More than their eyes could count. In their state of mind, the night sky was deeper than 3 dimensions. Crossing the Universe was a red void of stars, silhouette of the Moon. To create movement, the Cosmos sent out in all directions, shooting Comets.

Red was first out before sunrise in perfect 6' waves, 6 in a set. There was a time during that 3 day session when Red rode the first wave in that machine like 6 wave set and paddled the circular water current created by the squall back out to the waves. In the first wave he did a power full tail-edge slide out of the crescent of salt water. Taking the storms energy and current for speed, he tail-turned and paddled into the last wave. What choreography, what since of brotherhood, the other Surfers also caught waves in that 6 wave set.

They worked as a team, for survival. Tex and Red as fishermen, Dapper as camp 'cookie' and Slim as the gopher-beach comber-wood-scout.

The fishermen supplemented the diet of Dapper's 'foil fish Veracruz' with a choice of fish. Between Tex and Red, they were able locate pockets, schools, of fish including good eating sand bass, halibut, and a special find, parrot fish. High tide brought the fish closer to the shore and they could be seen swim-surfing in the hollows of tubing shore break waves all during the squall.

"1200 hours, Red, high tide, Parrot fish spotted, request the use of the 'Hawaiian sling'. Tex knew that Red liked to surf at high noon. He also knew that the fish were mesmerized by Red's surfboard fin trails in the waves as they reflected off the light rays of the noonday hot tropical hurricane squall. It was Ludie who was first aware that the fish had begun to ride the shore break which at times reached 4'. The schools, some were mixed specie, were hunting desert sand grubs wash up by the high tides.

"Permission Granted," sea lion-barked the Legendary Surfer. His huarache sandal heels thumping, he gives a surfers-water-mens salute of left hand out to the left, fluke-hand down, bend at the elbow- thumb in ear.

The barnacle and coral eating parrot-fish was a taste of delicacy not savored fresh by many humans other than the natives in the tropical regions of ring of fire. The method in which they were brought to the table for consumption made them very special to the 4 surfers that evening. Nate found that the best, surest way to spear them with the Hawaiian sling was to launch the rubber tubing sling shot like cord cocked behind the elbow and letting go the spear rod's tension while body-surfing the wave behind the fish, he using swim fins. As he speared one of the wiggling delicacies, he stood up in waist deep water and pitch forked the tropical colored fish up on the sand of shore. The sand having been created by the hard beaks of the fish chomp-grinding the calcium created by the coral and shellfish having been in existence for millions of years.

It was during one of these meals that Red told the others about a place in the Baja that he found on the Pacific side that had waves that broke like a machine and he had ridden for a mile. "The best wave in California!" He said.

Tex told his story on one of the nights about the Navel inquiry. About wandering since the Sub nightmare. But not about Kelly.

"Hey? How did you get here?" Slim is looking around the cove. "Don't you have transportation?"

CHAPTER 8

Long Ride Home

It was a time, a rare moment that happens during an 'El Nino' season that can last for a 1/2 day to sometimes 3 days, here, around the village. Cooling swells of clouds begin to form long before the first light of dawn. They are seen as gray puffs as if they are the breath of Odin, the darker ones will bring with them a misty squall from their inception along the equator, far out beyond the horizon of the sea. They pick up energy from the warming currents and release moisture vapor when the dew point is saturated. A few of the darkest clouds release on the town a fine refreshing moisture, a relief on this day in this region. It is a time when the air and land is cooler than the clouds. A time when the ocean is warmer than the sand.

Dapper is lost in his mind, as he is most of the time, and he attributes the situation to a time in his life for reflection. His surf friends remind him to not reflect back in time too long. Red said and the others agreed, "At our age we need to focus on whats in front of us. That, what is in front is the drama, the perils, the cautions and tribulations we must face and create a solution. To reflect on the past is looking at what has already happened."

"A person is only then looking for a better way to handle the situation if it ever appears again in the future," thought The Poser.

"Whataya look-en at?"

The question brought Dapper out of his trance and the dialect brought The Poser to answer, "Rainbows."

The surfer turned to the woman's voice and his old heart sored into a smile as bright as this fresh morning sun. "Marylou!?"

With a creak from the old pier's railing he twirled from his sea view and pushed himself with his back and torso towards her like a roped prize fighting boxer and with poise, he wrapped his tanned arms around the aged woman's now fragile shoulders.

She embraced him just above his rib cage and below his shoulder blades just as naturally and squeezed his back surfing muscles with her feminine hands like only a woman can do.

There was an impulse and they both felt it, but before their eyes met, Dapper gave her a proper Mexican greeting of affection. He came close to her ear and smacks his lips with a sound of a kiss. A sound not tawdry. He couldn't resist though, and he placed his long whiskered cheek to hers.

She couldn't resist either, and finding only an Earnest Hemingway whiskered face, she kissed his right ear lobe.

Their eyes met and in an instant, long remembered images spun and danced in their minds like rays of light in a carnival of sunsets from Maui.

They let go of their embrace as a mild temperature breeze from the sea brushed their hair, and a sea gull sunning himself on a pier pole squawked rambunctiously sending from his body a splatter on the ocean.

"Ya always been chasing them 'Rainbows' haven't you." She smiled her 'dock-girl' smile still showing her own teeth.

The word was all over the small beach town in Connecticut. "Dapper was home!" And Marylou knew where to find him.

"Ya been to the Tavern yet?"

"Na." He spent the first few days with his family and would soon take care of business in New York.

"Well come by. The guys want to see you." She was checking out his tanned face with the deep wrinkles in the corners of his eyes. The eyes looking like a sea turtle squinting at the horizon, seeing wave swells on a sun dappled sea. She noticed his now white hair was pulled back into a braided rope design held in place by a tooled leather sleeve with the image of a flying pelican, buttoned together twice by two polished natural jade stones.

"Of course, tonight. Is that alright? Thank for the invite." He smiled his perfect human smile. He knew what night was best for his long time surfer-fishermen friends. He would not want to miss this moment with long time comrades, the people he grew up with.

A fresh breeze tumbled across the warm deck of the fishing dock permeating of tar and old fish. It was strong enough to blow The Poser's hair over his left shoulder and also lift up Marylou's ankle long loose hippie printed gypsy dress, puffing up her ample bosomed filled bodice with nipple erecting cold air that was released through the crease in her cleavage.

"Well!" She exclaimed with a giggle, "I'll see you then."

Dapper chuckled also. He never missed the wind's antics. "Yeah!"

"She hasn't changed a bit," he said to himself.

Yes, a long time ago there was an amorous relationship between the two. They were young. His family never said anything, but their eyes said things from time to time. A family knows how a person is and they all know better than to meddle into the life created by this young man known as Dapper. The cousins and his sister grew up with him. His relatives remember when he was a child. The small town watched him also. The older ones don't think he ever matured. They think he never left the culture created in the sixties.

One thing is undeniably true and cannot be refuted even by the narrow minded, dollar sign blinded, money making culture that dictated his family; he too could accumulate money.

His family gave him a high school graduation present, a trip to Hawaii for the summer. They hoped it would break up his relationship with Marylou.

"And Daniel, when you come back in the Fall you will buckle down and go to Cornell," his father told him.

He didn't come back that Fall. He stayed on the North Shore of the Hawaiian Island called Oahu through it's winter waves. In his mind he obeyed his father and enrolled at the University in the spring.

Marylou missed him terribly and he missed her also. The family was surprised to find out that upon his return he still had enough money saved to rent an apartment off campus. Enough money to invite her to Cornell to live with him. She eventually got a job as a waitress. They went to the

Islands every winter which began a rift that was ever widening with his family.

"What? I'm going to school." He would explain to his Father.

In the Spring of his college graduation year, it took him six years to get to this point in his life, he had taken enough scrutiny from the family. Daniel stood toe to toe with his Father one afternoon. The day was filled and climaxed with a dinner party honoring Daniel's younger cousin who was three years younger than him. He was graduating from the same University. Daniel's father was making snide remarks to his brother as if Dapper was not there.

"Well brother, at least you only had to pay tuition for four years."

"Only three years. My son graduated early," said the brother.

"I've already paid for six!" declared Daniel's father. "Oh well, less inheritance for my boy I guess," shrugged the wealthy man.

Perhaps it was the sea lion instinct he had picked up while dealing with aggressive surfers. The Poser retorted, "Why don't you give me this year's intuition and I'll show you I can make money in this family also. In fact, I'll pay back all the college money you paid before my cousin does.

Everybody got a big laugh from that outburst. Daniel happened to be standing in view of the large full length mirror that adorned the visitor's hall and he saw The Poser, wearing Farney sunglasses on top of his head, tanned, with a long shag haircut, wearing white-tight Bermuda shorts and jap-slap scandals. And he was looking back at him. Dapper laughed too.

"Timing is everything." The Poser knew this better than most.

"Father," it was two days after the formal family get together and Daniel was in his Father's office at the local bank. The silver haired, white collar and tie attired man looked up and lowered his glasses in surprise to see his son occupying the work place. Dapper had his stylish Farney sunglasses perched above his eyebrows and on top of his head. Their blue eyes met.

"Dad I'm serious. Call it a loan if you want. I need start up capitol for a business."

The long time financier gave the lad a straight lipped disingenuous smile and lowered his eyes to his paperwork. "And what's in it for me as a loaner of capitol? You won't be leaving school."

"Your money back in 2 years."

The Father says nothing and doesn't look up. "With the family's usual 10% interest." Sitting at his ornate walnut desk, the clothing tycoon pooches his lips.

"And bragging rights," The Poser adds.

The spectacled man's eyebrows peer over the top rim of his gold wire rimmed glasses, "What kind of business? Not making surfboards I hope."

"No, a clothing line, same as you."

Father and Son did share a common trait. They were financial gamblers.

Still not looking up from the paper strewn desk, his eyes shift to a small antique wooden toy rowboat perched, half buried, in the day's paper chaos. The corners of his mouth indent with a creased crescent. "OK, I'll give you one year's intuition."

The elder's remark about surfboards brought out the sea lion again. "I need two years of intuition. I'm paying back in two years." Dapper gambles.

The Father is impressed with his Son's frankness. "OK." And he quickly stares into his offspring's eyes.

The Poser stood erect with his chin out and his arms to his sides. He placed his hands, outstretched behind like the flight feathers of a sea albatross. His eyes focused back like a tiger shark, "I need two years away from Cornell. He pauses. "When I'm successful, I'll go to graduate school." He gambled.

The white collared man turned his gaze towards a large original painting of an 18th century clipper ship named Cuttysark and chuckled to himself. "Graduate school?.. Too much rope could hang you."

The man had a gift for having things on this planet go his way. "You pull this off son and you won't have to go to graduate school," he said to himself.

"I'm going to New York tomorrow." Dapper's mother doesn't look up. "I have some business." She looks over her plastic horn-rimed glasses at the old surfer. "Tonight I'm seeing the guys at the Tavern."

"Well don't stay out too late." She focuses on her ornate antique Ming Dynasty tea cup. "I hear New York is dangerous." The blue printed cup and saucer clinkity-clink as she daintily sips her Olong Jasmine tea with shaky hands.

"It's two hours to sunset. I'll be on my way." He smiles a 'maybe smile' looking a bit like a cockatoo bird.

"Will you be alright by your self?" she has been alone since her husband died. It's been 2 years now. She doesn't acknowledge about the Tavern.

"I miss the rhythm-shuffle of surf sandals on a white pine floor." Dapper smiled. Red used to say that.

He took the coast route from the family mansion on the point to town and then to the old whaling wharf in the middle of the small crescent bay. It was built in the 1600's as the town hall and was converted into a full time Tavern in the late 1700's. It's longevity is a testament to old growth locust-wood. This bar has been a 'hang-out' for Dapper's generation since they were of age to partake in the presence of 'John Barleycorn'.

The wharf creaked as his sandals slip-stride over the crevices between the stout timbers. There were still a few black locust-wood mooring cleats used 200 years before to cinch the small mighty oak-wood sail ships to the docks, they are 3' diameter tourist attractions now. The sea birds like to roost on them also.

The Poser stopped to enjoy the company of a lone fisherman casting his lead sinker and clam bait over the rail of the horse-shoe pier that surrounded, on three sides, the small building perched out to sea. The wool pee-coated old salt found an opening in the kelp and dropped the leader there with a small splatter of sea rings.

"Oh, hey!" they both said simultaneously upon setting eyes. The Poser gazed into the chauffeur's 5 gallon bucket like a sea gull with his wings back and his webbed toes pointed slightly towards in. In the bucket were 2 small herring.

"Used to be two fish would feed both me and the wife. Captain Jack wants to know what you want to do with the 'Mitchel-25'.

Captain Jack and Dapper's Father were a cockpit crew during World War Two. Somehow, the two were able to salvage, buy, and, through the years, to restore this 1943, once heavily cannoned, escort-Boeing-25. (It now maneuvers in the sky like an Osprey Eagle for war memory tourists, and lighter without the weaponry.)

"I'm going to New York tomorrow. Can you have the Packard Wagon ready by six AM? Thanks for the 'heads up' on the plane. Are you coming in for grog?"

"Na, can't drink no more." Their eyes, creased around the edges, meet, and they smile together. "Have one for me Dapper. OK, six AM. My son Joe Jr. Is in there though."

"Ah!" His pole jerks and dips once, twice and with the third, he sets the hook with a upward yank of the pole. Rhythmically and keeping tension on the line with the bounce of the sinker while turning the reel handle, the fish is brought to a well versed height, leaving enough line between the pole tip eye and the fish. This, having been done many times, times too many to count, is climaxed with a boom-like motion over the rail into the bucket. "See you tomorrow at six Dap. I've got to get home. She says before dark."

And the lights come on with a yellow glow above the pier.

The Poser casually, but quickly pulls his German forged pocket knife out and makes a small incision in the fishes jaw cartilage and removes the hook. "See you." He puts the blade away and turns his head to the Tavern door. Taking a step in that direction, he pivots his neck towards the shore and again, sea gull-like he squawks, "Say hi to the wife." The fisherman chuckles as Dapper opens the old heavy bar door.

Dapper's impeccable timing changed the Tavern's dim daylight interior to a golden bronze blaze color as it radiated off the glass bottles of booze from the rays created by the day's sunset through the full length glass wood mullioned windows facing the sea. There were a few young fishermen numbing their leg and arm muscles with grog and one sea going bearded old timer mumbling his mind on hard liquor. They look over as a breeze comes in when the door is opened.

The Poser sees a familiar silhouette leaning on the bar and he shuffles over like a rooster, putting himself belly-up in the sunset warmth with the young fisherman on his left. "Margarita." He puts a $50 bill down. "And a round for the house." Everyone's head lifts a bit higher.

"Dapper! Is that you?" says the old-timer, "The sea hasn't swallowed you up yet?"

"I'm Joe's Son," says the Bar Keep, extending his callused hand across the bar. "You want a Margarita?" he said it as if he had to remember how to make it.

"Yeah, with 2 lime slices and a dash of sugar." And with a second thought, "just a half jigger of your best Tequila, not stirred." A set of waves bounced off the bottom of the wharf giving it a low thunderous shake.

"I'm Jack," the young fisherman standing to the left of the old surfer extends his callused hand in friendship to the town legend. His bare arms are covered in the tight tattoos of his generation, extending the entire length of both arms and resembling a long sleeve paisley shirt from the generation before.

"Are you Captain Jack's Grandson?" Dapper raises his eyes from the colorfully ink scratched arms and looks into the young man's 'Outer Banks Hanks' sun glasses. "Call me Dapper." The Bar Keep puts down an old, well used short tumbler cocktail glass with no napkin for the pony-tailed surfer with Javan simulated tortoise shell, wrap-around prescription fish-eye, photo-chromic sun glasses. He uncaps a lager beer for the fishermen. "Thanks for remembering the salt." Dapper raises his glass to all in attendance.

"Arr!!!" they all roar in unison as if to be heard over a roaring, wind-shrieking ocean storm.

"So Jack, you're a Fisherman?" Dapper sets down his half glass of drink along with the thump from metal tankards of drawn ale set down onto the old wooden tables.

"Yeah, I fish alone. Are you still surfing?"

"Yep, it's still my main function." Dapper raises his glass once more and clinks the young man's drinking vessel, "To the sea!"

"Arr!" they all say and laugh heartily.

The Poser takes a swallow, "Jack, tell me a sea story."

The heavy weathered oak front door of the Tavern creaked from a low lying gust of wind from the sea, bringing with it a 6' shore wrapping set of 5 waves that rocked the pilings of the wharf and vibrating the white pine wood floor of the old meeting hall. The Tavern entry door, salvaged from a shipwreck on an island in Nova Scotia, creaked, opened, and let in a fresh breeze permeating of 'Panache-Musk' perfume and a silhouette of a woman who was recognized by all. It was her curves that raised the guy's squinting eyes.

"He caught a Marlin Dapper." She slides in between the two sea men at the belly bar as they smoothly one-step-slide apart a 1/2 a bar stool in opposite directions. She makes sure all three are touching through her.

"You caught..caught a Marlin? When? The old retired Boson's Mate lifts himself up straight and bows his head to peer into the sun as it silhouettes through the amber bottle of now almost empty brew.

"Last week." Jack's Grandson glances at the gray bearded Boson, scans around for the other's approval, and then at Dapper. When he knew he had the attention of everyone, and the floor of the poop deck...

"It was a nice day with green swells on a blue sea, sunny, with no breeze. The marlin was floating on the surface with it's dorsal fin in the warm sunshine." The tattooed young man left early, before sunrise, before the night lights of the wharf turned off with the light of day.

"The sword beaked brute never heard me. Must have been asleep or day dreaming." Captain Jack's grandson caught sight of the fin before the beast heard or felt the drone of the single screwed trawler, and the lad maneuvered his boat into a drift towards the fish.

"I got close enough to use my stubby pole and heavy shark line." Plunk; Jack III drew the attention to wakefulness the slumbering fish with a lure made of African jungle-cock feathers. Jack reeled it in.

"I put my second cast 20 yards to the South, close enough to a floating debris pile." The angler let the feathers drop to a guessed depth of 3 feet. The sail began to amble towards the pile of floating sea weed still not noticing the trawler.

"The fish went into stalking mode quick." The fisherman side stepped along the deck and maneuvered the jig towards a patch of brilliance on the sea from rays of the now appearing morning sun. The now mesmerized stalker took a fast dive.

"I reeled a bit faster and that fish took the lure through the sunrise and out to sea." The tattooed arms set the hook and let the fish go for around 150 yards.

"I didn't want him too far out so I started working the reel-drag a little to let him know who was boss." The lone fisherman began to maneuver his body to a good fish landing spot which also held the gaff.

"The tourist fishing boat was on it's way out by this time and I could see it was heading right for me. I didn't want the fish spooked by the engines so I started man-handling the beast in." The Marlin was large and heavy but lazy, and didn't give much of a fight until it reached the side of the trawler and then got spooked by the charter boat. Jack let it swim for about 100 yards. He set the drag a few notches more and began to man handle the tiring sword back to his boat.

"I hollered at Charlie if he would gaff the fish for me." Jack looked around the bar room and then at Dapper. He smiled courteously at Marylou. "Charlie is a deck-hand on the tourist boat." The young tattoo-armed fisherman reaches for his bottle of beer but the amber bottle is empty.

Joe junior smiles as Dapper puts another $50 bill on the belly-up and slides it to the chauffeur's son, the Barkeep.

"Another round," says the old surfer. "Belly up for a stein you sea sick sea slugs!"

Jack III has his back to the bar, standing, leaning on his spider webbed tattooed elbows. "The captain of the tourist boat wouldn't let the deck-hand help me. Said it was against insurance rules."

Joe hands a tray of filled old metal draft schooners and scones to Marylou and makes 2 margaritas putting a jigger-plus of tequila absentmindedly in each double glass.

"You know I would have helped you if I could, Jack," hollered Charlie from somewhere in the room.

Joe turned to face the bar crowd and handed the two lime cocktails to Dapper. He looked the tanned surfer in the sunglasses and winked. "Yeah sure Charlie."

"The Captain gunned the charter boat and sped about 20 yards out but within sight of the drama. The movement spooked the fish and it swam away from me again." Youth has a wonderful mechanism for youthful warriors. They have no idea of body fatigue and they think they are invincible. Jack took control of the pole and line and snugly lured fish at 75 yards.

Marylou, with a waft of perfume sat back down between the men. She clinked glasses between the three. Dapper put his arm around the woman's waist. "So, did you bring the marlin in?"

"Sure he did!" Marylou puts her hand on the old surfer's thy and...

Jack smiles over her shoulder. "Charlie the least you could do is fillet that beast up and cook us some marlin steaks and fries."

Charlie is up in a flash and bumps his table, "where's the knife?"

"C'mon you cactus and fruit tot-lier," George II raises his pewter mug which it's froth linings show he is down to his last swallow, "drink like a seaman and have a brew with us."

"And tell us a Surfer's sea story." George slid his empty tankard along the bar top. It deftly missed the warn-smooth grooves in the aged old growth spalded maple 2" bar top. The empty vessel slid shuffle-board style past Marylou and the Poser bringing the voluptuous woman to her feet as the pewter came within a hair width of her bosoms.

"Cold glasses for everyone!" she brushed her protruding nippled Alpaca sweater along the old surfer's wrinkled neck and straitening, lengthening his braid, slightly.

"Sure, let me get some air first." And The Dapper stands, he slides his fingertips along the top of the woman's hand and touches the inside of her left wrist. His neck is in the opposite of feelings compared to the hair raising adventures his mind conjured, remembered, concerning images in the wilds of the Baja.

The Poser returned to his bar stool recollecting how fortunate he was not to be concerned about keeping a seat in a crowded bar. He missed the remote Cantina. The jaunt took him longer than in his younger years. "Oh yeah, I took in the night sky." He was back into the murmur of the Tavern before all cold glass mugs of draft were served.

"It was the time of the 'Spring Equinox"- and the murmuring subsided.

"The swell took 4 days to arrive and break as an 'A-frame' on a large flat slab of granite located 1/2 a day from civilization." Civilization? The closest village was nothing more than a dusty gas stop for freight trucks, with petrol, a Tienda with beer, and a small cardboard-walled Casita con Comida.

Marylou placed the last cold draft in front of The Poser. They clinked the antique Chek Republic glass mugs. Dapper's insides ached for more than one reason. The Tavern Waitress pointed her thumb towards the heavy-beamed archway with double doors, made from ship storm hatches square-latticed with 1 inch oak, which separated the kitchen. She would help with the swordfish.

"Red was there. So was his brother Slim, and Tex."

A raucous sound of approval was heard along with the thump of 16 once handled schooners on the table tops. They knew Red. He handled his steel slide guitar here many times. There was a moment of silence not rehearsed. They knew he was gone, or those that didn't were told in a whisper.

"We were in the Buick." Dapper was referring to the 1947 four wheel drive 'Woodie Roadmaster' that Red won in a Southern California surf contest in the late 60's.

"The surf landed on shore at seven feet," said The Poser. Dapper reached for the beer and his insides throbbed in a dull pain. He withdrew his hand.

"We were in four wheel drive, we placed the gears with a rocking grind just 1/2 mile from the village. We crossed 2 creeks." The water flowing over the cobble and ice-cooler sized smooth rocks is more dangerous when it rains in the Gigantor mountains that form the center backbone of the Baja peninsula. "We forged the two creeks one day before the equinox and set up camp at 'The Slab'. The rain came that night.

"Red had his 'Edwards Style' tinted red three stringer and the guys were riding the newer shaped 'Shroasme' 7'2's. Tex brought the latest designed 'Squash-Tail-Tri'."

"A soggy camp has a way of getting one up early. The sound of pounding surf excites a surfer out of sleep. The roar of a swollen river over large boulders excites an adventurer.

A 'Westie'... in this part of the world, in the Eastern Pacific Rim, is a storm that is a slip-slide affair. It has a distinct direction, East, along the latitude of the Sun and over Mt. Fuji, but the cold winds from the Asian Highlands will vary the typhoon's location on the sea. The warm Baja Chubasco wind Entity and the Canadian prairie wind Entity called Maria will battle for the storms energy created in Asia.

"One never knows how much water will come out of those Baja mountains after a storm and as far as we knew, we were the only ones who knew about this surf spot. No one was aware we where there." The hair on the old surfer's neck stood up again. He took a long swig of draft lager and smiled at everyone. "It was day two and we surfed all day. We could stay one more night. We had supplies for three days and two nights."

The smell of fish and chips wafted from the galley. Dapper eyed the glass schooners on the patron's tables. They were full.

The surfers actually only got 3 sessions in. The tides played a big part in the form of that Asian beast of a wave. They all got adrenaline flowing rides on the fast, thick lipped squares.

"Red had a standout wave. The difficulty being his long board. His large, 6'4" framed wide stance gave him the advantage of more board rail in the wave face but the wood single fin would scrape the bolder reef in order to escape the pitching bowl breaking in sometimes no water at low tide. His wave, at medium tide, was conquered with a rail grabbing switch stance, knees buckled and planted one on each outside stringer. His back held up the pitch of the wave. He did a full-body tuck out the back-door of the dark blue 8' Chubasco offshore wind blown slab of a wave just before the barrel made it's run for the shore."

"Slim broke his board in the second session. He paddled out when the tide was too low. We had deep and long single fins on our 7'2" drawn out rounded pins. They were sending up coral and large barnacles off of the reef-slab also." Slim's pelvis bounced off the reef also and we would find out later the rock slab cracked it.

Dapper whispered to MaryLou as she began to walk plates of Marlin and fried potatoes around. "A pitcher of draft at each table. Ah..no more for me."

He slips two more $50 bills to Joe the barkeep.

"That 'Tri-Fin' of Tex Ludie's was a standout. It did the best in paddling out and the fins were shorter. They never scraped the reef." There was not such thing of getting caught inside with this swell. The short faced waves never ceased. The paddle out zone was the rip caused by the river mouth which created on shore an obstacle in the path of civilization. What about the other river mouth 2 miles North was on all four of the wave rider's minds.

"The river water stopped rising around 5 fingers to sunset on that second day and that was the first ease of tension we felt in 3 days. Perhaps we were becoming acclimatised to the harshness that is known in the Baja." Dapper took a bite of swordfish. He reminisced chopping Mexican cabbage as the other campers prepared the salad of canned tuna, fried spam, and mayonnaise-paprika dressing. They added Frito's, and beer from the slushy-iced cooler.

"We all slept good that night under the stars. The twinkling of the Cosmos was our only source of light except for the glow of the smokey driftwood fire."

Dapper finished most of his meal. The Tavern began to fill a second mug of brew from their pitchers.

It took 6 hours of the first day for the wind to subside and most of the night to get the anger and turbulence out of the West Swell waves. The first blush of citrus, silver-blue hued raze of Sun revealed fine shaped 'A-Framed' waves with only a hint of wind, alternately from 3 directions on that third morning. And at high tide the waves subsided.

The surfers rode the tubing beauties through breakfast. They dried off and began the task of crossing the first of several creeks.

"The river didn't drop much in the night. We were hoping it would be a creek at first light. We tied the Buick's winch to Tex Ludie who crossed the boulders in butt deep water. That wasn't as deep as we thought. He tied the cable around a driftwood log washed down to the shore from the desert during the Fiji deluge and we crossed with the loaded vehicle, surfers and all. Ludie complained all day about having 'fisherman's ass' because of his wet trunks."

The surf never let up for 3 days and the high atmospheric wind currents blew the animated clouds from the Chinese prairies East, across the Pacific Ocean. And West, across the prairies of Canada and North America, they followed an ancient path created by the Sun's latitude arch over Mt. Fuji. A direction between volcanoes created long before there was an ocean or waves. It was the Baja-Chubasco entity that drew that ocean energy towards this shore.

"I never seen so many rocks. The tides of this storm took away all of the sand. That old Woodie was shimmy-shaking and wood swelling all the way to the next river which had boulders as big as Volkswagens in it." The Poser's eyes flashed, then he smiled.

Marylou set down two double shot glasses wafting of margarita. "A half shot of Mescal only." And she sat down. A fragrance of jasmine-musk permeated from her bosom and crossed the old surfer, bringing that wonderful feeling to the man's grizzled neck.

"We convinced Tex to run the cable out seeing as how he was already wet and had the job figured out. He was too busy in the boulders to notice as we took a pee and drank a Tecate in the shade created by the Buick Roadmaster. It took three separate winch connections to get across that low water river. That Woodie still creaks to this day from that trip."

"Hey! Everyone, it's been good to see you!" Dapper took his last swallow and put his tanned sinuous arm around Marylou...

CHAPTER 9

Reminiscing

It was late midmorning. In fact the Sun was a full hand with the thumb up past the flat horizon above the sea. It was the third morning since the party at the Tavern.

The Poser walked up a stretch of beach starting at sunrise and located the place of contemplation he remembered since he was a young 'grommet' surfer.

At this time of year the sand is mostly washed out to the kelp beds which are to be extracted of their accumulated Earthly nutriments by the turbulences of tides, currents, and storms.

Dapper was brought out of his thoughts about the last two days by the sound of the first wave surge of the incoming tide as it growled across the coble stones that were left on the beach instead of sand. There were random indentations between the piles of smooth, fist sized stones, whose colors ranged indefinitely with the hues of the planet including onyx-black and clear-quartz, most with specks of fool's gold. These undulating shore formations had places that were slightly below sea level, some with carpets of sand. They were about 3 yards in diameter, some were light color sand, some dark. In other sections the smooth beach cobbles were piled into raised mounds that peaked just above the last storm surge.

The incoming tide lapped over the cobbles into the sand pit in which Dapper sat in his backpack-folding chair. It, bringing a dark, wet, ambient changing sheen within inches of the beach man's feet and highlighting the colors of the stones. The gradual movement brought with it a slight breeze with it's waves and at his vantage point at sea level, the man was brought home to it's primal, Earthly, odor.

A pelican dropped it's flight into the predominate air current of the first set of tidal waves and, as it swept the air past The Poser in a fast moving wave curl, it focused for a quick moment into the Surfer's eyes with it's right eye. Then, looking down the line of the wave's air current that it was riding, it placed it's flight feather tips, three in all, about an inch into the wave face, creating a swishing sound audible to the old Surfer. Dapper, the 'birder', and member of the Audubon Society, let out a screech. The sea bird must have heard it because as the wave spent it's last energy, in a growling crash on the gravelly shore, the pelican rose into the wind-bubble of turbulence. And the moment between falling with the Planet's gravity or taking flight with it's wings, he held himself proudly and wiggled his tail feathers.

Dapper moved his chair to a higher elevation from sea level. He was glad to be back into familiar territory, back to his world, his reality. He spent the day before in New York seeing the family doctor.

His family was becoming intense with their insistence that he come back permanently and take care of the Family business. The finance logistics are run in the high rise district in New York.

The Doctor's appointment was Daniel's idea.

The man spent the day after the Tavern party nursing a slight hangover and conversing with his Elders. Most were closer to ninety years old than seventy but they didn't think so. They had become robots of the health system. Each were taking an excessive amount of around forty meds abuse. Their daily routine entailed the ingestion of one pill after another to combat the side effects of the last medication taken. Their physician visits were every other day except Friday, Saturday, and Sunday.

Through the conversation that evening, Daniel found a few parallels with his body dysfunctions and his family's ailments.

It was good fortune that the Surfer planned his physician appointment on an off day from his parent. The doctor had some influence in the decision also. It took some persuasion to convince Dapper's seniors that it was a good idea to go. The Family spokesman was not so sure. One of the primary reasons had to do with the vehicle Dapper was taking.

"You're not taking my Mercedes? That old wagon doesn't have a computer." He was referring to the 1941 Packard 120 Woodie Dapper's Grandfather bought new.

The Dapper was dressed impeccably in a dark sea-green corduroy suit with a phi-lo-blue colored freshly ironed, soft, long sleeved, 'chamois' shirt. He wore a silk, Windsor knotted, Gerry Garcia acid splashed tie, the pattern resembling a florescent blue-green wave, undulating in Space. And of course he wore his Venezuelan ostrage leather huaraches with Peruvian cashmere-wool, camel brown, socks.

Jerry's eye brows went up slightly and he reached for the freshly varnished wooden back passenger door's brass, intricately forged handle. The Poser chuckled and deftly opened the front door, he grabbed the embossed leather handle over the door with his right hand. He smoothly swung in and landed on the Cordovan maroon, leather-tooled, arched, overstuffed, passenger bench seat. The center arm rest was down.

Red rode in it. They freighted his acoustic, and electric steel-slide guitar to the Tavern in it.

The morning glow in the sky of blue just before the sunrise, looking like a Maxfield Parrish painting, brought out the dark blue with slight beer-amber colored gold flake paint on the Packard's long hood. That color also matched Dapper's shirt, but without the flake.

The engine's 'strait-eight' cylinders hummed along the two lane road under the hardwood trees. Occasionally a sign slowed the Woodie's progress and the vintage vehicle's clutch and shifter had to be used. The car was heavy and the brakes were an early design. "Are we going to the Firm?" Jerry liked this old Woodie and it showed by how smoothly he could shift it.

"Yeah, how's my cousin?"

"Hey look, a rainbow." The driver took a hand off of the big walnut steering wheel to point in the direction of prismatic light but quickly regained a two-handed grip to gain control of the huge, heavy, 120 inch chassis car with no power steering.

"Do you still surf?"

"Yeah, I once rode through a rainbow."

"Oh yeah."

The Poser skim-finned into the prism grabbing the outside rail of his surf craft with his left hand, and three-pronged with 2 feet, chevroned with heels touching, on the inside rail. He dragged his right palm along the wave face and knifed the boards nose through the rainbow. Everything and every color turned to a bright gold and that was all he could see. The rider was blind. He skimmed his back arm palm along the breaker to feel the velocity of the wave curl and used his right fingers like the flight feathers of a sea going avian.

And The Poser thought to himself, "Hand and fingers balanced with the nose curve of the board, tail for thrust. I hadn't thought about the mortal words of the deceased Surfer legend known as Red for a length of time."

"Yeah sure." Jerry was concentrating on his driving the 2 hours to New York, more than listening to Dapper. Besides, the traffic was becoming heavier and the drive more intense, now that the Woodie had left the upstate hardwood forest. Now the car lanes had doubled.

Dapper didn't notice, he was lost in one of his hangover day dreams. Perhaps it was the rhythm of engine head tappets and the hum of rocker bearings, along with the gentle squeak of ash body wood grown in these forests that rubbed in the ever expanding holes filled with stainless steel bolts forged in a foundry in Pennsylvania.

There was a smile to his face. The Poser was with Tex in his mind.

"Tex? Yeah I remember him. He's a birder too. Right? You two still surf together?" The chauffeur remembers shaking a heavily tattooed hand.

They were in the Baja a long time ago. They were in their prime. They had been on the road for 2 days. They watched cloud formations on the Southern horizon a days drive from the California-Mexican border. They camped by a river-mouth but were abruptly interrupted by a violent squall. They watched it come over the South-West horizon. In the form of a medium dark, silver-gray-blue, rolling, coarse forming wet mass of energy. The center opened with a transparent gold-orange light. Chubasco bellowed a challenge like a huge, roaring, tuba-trumpet, up the river valley and the sound echoed off the canyon boulders back to the sea. The squall began to pour rain. Enough precipitation to send the young Surfers packing to reach higher ground before the dirt trails became impossible to navigate even with four wheel drive.

They slip-slided to the paved highway and, traveling about 2 miles North, they wheeled their white 1969 Chevy Blazer into a cardboard walled, palm shingle thatched roofed, Cantina, looking for hot coffee.

"Hey look, Red's here!" the 40's era four-wheeler parked in the wet dirt gave the legend away.

Their clothes and long hair, still damp from the sudden downpour, and their feet and sandals, slopped with the red mud of the Baja; they were greeted with that known scowl of a Mexican woman. Who, in this instance, was the 'Patrona' of this Cantina. And she knew that red mud would not leave the casa easily.

Red took a sip of personally spooned Nescafe coffee. "Just because you two are surfers you don't have to be wet all the time." Then he said in Californio-Spanish, "Rosa, were is your mop. These 'caballeros' want to clean up after themselves.

Slim, Red's brother, belched low some of his breakfast and laughed his usual infectious greeting. "Look, a couple of sea sick sea slugs."

It was enough enjoyment to make even Rosa loosen up and she even smiled..slightly, as she set a hot bent up pan with a loose handle half full of boiling, steaming water on the wobbly table. "Use their spoons, we have no leche." They noisily drag two warn hand carved pine wooden chairs up to the only other table and she places two chipped and cracked, coffee stained, sand colored mugs and the jar of dried coffee crystals on to a white, stained, embroidered linen, place mat.

Slim slips a matchbook under the shortest leg of the table. "You guys, are you headed back to the States?"

"Don't use his spoon, he licked it." Red hands over his still wet coffee shovel.

"Where have you guys been?" the Poser hands the spoon to Tex. He ignores Slims question.

"Up at the Casas." Slim's belly gurgles loudly.

They all noticed that the rain had stopped.

Rosa came back for their order but was warded off and the two each laid a $25 centavo coin on the table.

All four slurp down their remaining freeze-dried coffee brews and go outside. Red is looking at the octopus-looking cloud formation on the Southern horizon as they all are. He surf-saunters over to the pink, crudely painted banyo 10 feet behind the Cantina.

"I don't think we're going to the U.S. yet." Tex quickly climbs into the motor running blazer and again looks at the sky.

Red steps away from the outhouse with a bit of white powder lye on a couple of toes. There is a squeak from the door-spring as it slams loudly. Slim fart-trots in that direction. Red waves at the mud throwing white Blazer.

"No! No!" Rosa flings herself off the back porch with the mop in her up-stretched hands and swinging it over her head. She says more in Spanish and chased Slim away from her personal banyo as if he were a goat in a corn field. She chased him all the way to the Woodie-Wagon and even gave him an under-handed, unwashed, whip like flip on his trunk backside with the braids of the mop head. Good thing the trunks were dirty anyway.

"Oh man I gotta go! Red, go back inside and distract her.. Ask her for a date."

"Ola Senorita.." Red waves his right hand covertly, behind his back and goes back inside the Cantina glancing at a crude Mexican sign advertising-'Dates For Sale'

That was Slim's cue, but he couldn't and didn't make it all the way to the hole in the boards. He picked out a cardboard box, found just out of sight of the highway and dropped his trunks. A heavy slam of the Woodie passenger door was Red's cue, and before he met Rosa's suspicious eyes, he said "Adios," and hot-foot-scampered to the driver's seat and pushed the floor peddle starter of the four-wheeler, Harmon Marmon Buick Roadmaster.

And yes, there was a sign crudely painted red on a wind weathered wooden watermelon crate that could be seen from the highway both from the North and from the South. There were fresh sticky dates, picked ripe from a remote oasis in the nearby rugged hills on a rancho owned by Rosa's family. The dates sweet, brown sugary-palm smell permeated her small restaurant, especially during hot days that lapped into the evening cool.

"Dates? You bought dates? In my condition?" Slim saw the desert sage reveal an off shore wind.

"Don't eat so many and Montezuma would leave your sweet ass alone." Red wheeled his off shore vehicle South knowing that with as few dirt fishermen's paths there were, the one with the white government sign post that had a '7' embossed on it should bring them to a cove known by the few Surfers who frequented this area.

The brothers were both aware that they would not ride alone at this surf spot, because, as soon as they left the highway kilometer marker stake, there were fresh tire tracks in the quick drying mud. They arrived in time to see the 2 East coast Surfers paddle out into 6' California-mellow waves shaped clean by a definite Baja desert offshore breeze. By the time the brothers suited up and waxed their boards, both Easterners had ridden a wave.

Red beat all three of the other Surfers in a paddle out and pivoted the tail of his Phil Edwards personally shaped long board, and, taking 3 deep lunged inhales in rapid succession, he took off on a fine, clean roller. He bottom-turned late, in order to let the other guys get over the slow moving face, and then, with his large body wide stance, he did a full rail turn with that 9'8" surf craft. The Legend walked to the nose of the board and back twice, and, riding the wave to the beach in respect for the squall that delivered it, he did a tail-pivoting stand-up kick-out and grabbed the nose rails.

"So, did Tex see you ride through the rainbow?" Jerry pulled The Poser out of his surf trance.

"Huh! Oh no."

The sky went brooding with dark clouds about an hour or two later. As the squall moved North from the cove, the waves subsided and in their place came more rain.

Dapper now noticed the intensity of the traffic and they neared New York.

"Now you got me curious. You better get on with this 'rainbow-ride'. We'll be at the office high rise in thirty minutes.

30 minutes, 60 minutes, maybe longer, the rain came down. Both vehicles headed North, in sight of each other and they found a channel on their CB's using the handles- East Coast and California. They passed up the rain and they got in front of the telltale swirling cloud mass on the horizon in time to catch the swell 2 hours before dark at a fine surf break in Ensanata. Three other surfers were in the line up making a total of 7 in the water riding again, perfect waves. One of the 3 commented that the swell began to break about 3 hours earlier.

All caught beautiful rides, but Tex Ludie's was the standout. It was late in the evening and the wave faces became a light chatter, the color of green ink, dark, making Ludie's tattoos blend with the still beautiful curling breakers as they moved across the horizon into this natural Mexican jetty. Then, as they became thinner in the shallower water, the hue became the color of a transparent olive, silhouetting Tex.

The ominous color of the sea as well as the ominous gray of the clouds in the sky sent the others to the shore. They know the down pour of precipitation is inevitable.

Tex paddles hard and drops down the 'A-frame' face, standing up quickly. He turns his Mactavish shaped 8'6" midway down the chattering, slightly cross-wind blown face of algae-green ink, made transparent by the setting sun. The off shore wind dies off and is replaced with the first drops of rain. Without the wind to hold it back, the wave becomes a wall 40 yards long and Tex Ludie takes a full inside rail run for the wave's shoulder which he makes but has to perform the wave riding maneuver known as 'A full-body-Islander' pull out.

"If the ocean was a woman and I was a duck, I'd dive to her bottom and never come up." In Ludie's mind, the wave was trying to devour him. He lets it engulf his body as a sacrifice to the Earth's wave God, Daga, to appease it's appetite. With his spirit from the Heavens, he wills his wave craft out through a weakness on the inside vortex of cosmic energy created in the Earths salty H2O, as it suck-vacuums the ocean floor for nutrients.

"Tex caught the best one in that secession. We drove North, across the border to 'Trestles' and spent the night covertly, on the beach. The four of us paddled out in the dark, before sunrise, in order to be the first to see waves. Ten other Surfers were in the outside water lineup before we saw waves." Dapper startled as a horn from the New York traffic honked the driver's impatience. "I caught the 'rainbow-wave' there."

The Poser let on as though the ride was the only one through a rainbow but, the truth be told, it was a start of an obsession with him that would last to this day.

"Every thing turned to gold." "We rode 'Rincon' and then 'Santa Cruz' with that squall before it dissipated."

The Packard Woodie slows with the clutch and two gears, then turns right. The brakes gently squealed to a stop in the underground parking lot of the 'skyscraper' building housing the office of The Dapper's family business.

CHAPTER 10

Get Me Home

He raises his face out of the sand that is still damp from the night's high tide. The abrupt sugar-donut-facial takes his mind away from the vacation's drama with his physician in New York. "I'm getting weak."

"Na, I'm letting New York distract me.. From my yoga," he says out loud. And he goes into a form called by some Surfers as the 'Scouts Awareness'. He deliberately looks with intense focus first North, towards town 2 miles, and then South, along the beach wilderness park. Someone is coming from both directions. He recognizes them as a third entity reveals itself, the Sun comes from behind a low lying cloud on the Eastern horizon, at first giving golden rays over the top of a lavender cloud as the orb of unfathomable heat rises above it.

In a cat-like Tai-Chi form, The Poser maneuvers gracefully, but with muscles taunt, holding his body in a regal upright posture, tight as a stone. His out stretched arms and hands, though tight, appear as feathers, and he brings them in front toward the Sun in greeting as if he were touching the out stretched new day's rays of light with his whole body, through his finger nails.

Then the man touches his finger tips and tilts his out stretched wrists inward and stares intently, with eyes closed, at the intensely bright heat through the flanges and thumb triangle funneled through his palms.

The Poser breathes through his nose deeply, as if the Sun's energy came through his palms, and the man directed it into his heart and he held his breath. He looks down at the sand.

"I'm not going there," he tells his body.

Instead, he swivels his head like a Rapture and stares with clear focus at the figure-silhouette approaching from the South. He breathes in the sea breeze as it pushes the cloud on the horizon West, in front of the rising morning Sun. And the cloud changed to a blushing pink as it headed West, making the warming orb appear to move behind it.

"A swell is coming."

The Poser pivots his up stretched neck and focuses, bird-like, with his heart feeling like a dove. He breathes in and releases his finger tips towards the figure coming his way from the North, from town.

With his out stretched arms and swiveling hips, knees, and feet, he scans the horizon as the Sun's rays glows the color of a male salmon in heat through the bottom of the now red clouds. Turning the ocean an undulating hue of jade.

"You been sleeping on the beach again? You shouldn't, it's too cold." She arrived first. "You got sand in your hair." She came close. Between Dapper and the ocean and took the back of his neck softly. Her voice was like the cooing of a dove to it's mate. And she brushed off the sand on his thinning white hair.

The wind, a chilly one, wrapped around the two lifting her long rather heavy weave cotton and hemp dress and his cannoneir's braided-tail, slightly. Bringing with it the musky fragrance of her perfume and it twirled around them.

"Was that you that I saw face down in the sand a while ago?" Jerry, the chauffeur, has great vision. He too wipes the shore particles off the top of Dapper's left ear.

The Poser is now out of his Tai-Che trance.

All three absent mindedly sit in the sand, just above the tide line. In a small canyon with walls of sandstone carved out by a relentless wave that all three know has been here since at least as long as these old timers remember.

The Poser is watching sets of perfectly formed blue-green swells of three, peel off brilliant white foam along the pebble and coarse sand beach. A rainbow is formed at the same place along the wave by the angle of rays appearing as from a three phalanger expanse of of fingers, on an outstretched hand and arm held horizontally from Daga and laying in midair between the horizon and bottom of the golden orb. Yeah, The Poser.. Tex Ludie would have understood.

"Dapper?" Her soothing, gravely-bourbon voice brings The Poser out of his surf moment. She and the chauffeur glance at each other perhaps a little nervously.

"Yeah" The old Surfer notices a stick about 12 inches long and about a 2 inch diameter, floating, and heading out to sea. It is just making itself over the top of the steep faced dark transparent jade waves. The beach's backwash is propelling the wood away from shore. He doesn't take his eyes and focus off of the flotsam.

"We want to talk business," a voice comes to The Poser's other ear.

"What kind of business." The Dapper looks over at his long time friend and then back at the stick that is now moving closer to shore, on the surge from the sea, with still perfectly wrapping 3' shore pound.

A waft of musky, Indian-Hindu perfume from the other side of The Poser is tantalizing as it is sucked up the face and curl of an incoming set of waves. The stick is hurled from the top of the predominate wave and pitched toward the shore hitting stones and then swallowed up by a foaming shore pound.

"We want to form a clothing line that will be biodegradable."

Temporarily, The Poser releases his focus, but, regains it when he searches and locates with his mind, the stick. It is deposited in a small pile of fist sized cobbles grouped before the small cove inlet.

A set came and went, reaching all the way to the sandstone cliff. The stick was gone.

"A fabric," came a voice in one ear.

"With some kind of bi-product that feeds the planet," came the female voice in the other ear.

The Poser notices the stick and it's now back out, in between the breaking waves and shore. Back where he first saw it. "I'll have to confer with 'Captain Nemo'."

"I'll get back to you guys." Dapper stands up and looks out to sea. The two on either side of him frown and shrug their shoulders at each other behind his back.

The Poser sees the stick is heading in a current that has begun to move South. He turns, Tai-Che like, on his toes and ankles, to face Mary Lou and offers his out stretched arms and hands to help her up from the sandy mound on the cobble strewn shore. A breeze offers the men a glimpse of her silky purple panties.

"Can you take me to the airport tomorrow?" Dapper gently lifts his former intimate friend to her feet. He feels a pain deep in his chest.

"Are you going to Southern California? Sure, early, maybe 5:00 AM? I need to take my wife for a doctor's appointment here, in town, in the after noon." The chauffeur stands, and they all begin walking North, towards the wharf.

"Doctor- is Amie OK?" A shore-pound wave roars gravelly and soaks their feet from behind, but it does not drown out the concern in The Dapper's voice.

Jerry's wife grew up with all of them.

"Oh, you didn't know? Amie fell in the rocks last year." Mary Lou and Amie were close friends.

"Yeah, a rouge wave got both of us right back there." Jerry remembers painfully. The moment would end the couple's walks on the beach for ever.

She had remarked about seeing a pearl-white stone resembling a skull and they both bent over to gaze at it with their backs to the surf. The 4 waves crashing force swept them both off their feet. The chauffeur got to his feet fairly quickly for his age and reached out to help his spouse. The look on her face and the helplessness at her appendages confirmed that she was injured.

"No! No, not yet," she put her arms around his neck. "Aw-not yet!"

He looked far, up and down the beach, and there was no one there. "Let me see if this will help," and with her arms around his neck, he puts his arms under her arm pits. "I have two words to say to you that might motivate you- 'Life-Flight."

It took less than a minute for her to vision herself spinning in a life saving gurney, 40' in the air, all the way to the town hospital. With all of the inhabitants to gawk at her ride in the sky.

They both rose up-right out of the cobbles and, looking back at the indentation of her body in the wet sand, was a double-fist size stone where her lower spine had been.

Amie is a tough Native American and she endured the pain long enough for the chauffeur to get her to the town doctor.

"She's a semi-invalid now," Jerry wipes a tear from his eye and smiles unconvincingly at Dapper. "She uses a cane and a wheelchair."

"I'll be back in time." Again, a fake smile comes to his face. The smile happens much of the time now.

The pain comes to Dapper's chest again. Not quite center, but deep inside behind his sternum.

"We're going to Roswell airfield. I bought the 'Mitchel-25'. Captain Jack is flying me to Baja California Sur, Mexico."

That brought a genuine smile to Jerry. The smile made the chest pain diminish. Dapper put his right arm around Mary Lou. So did the other man with his left arm, and she smiled, creating a glow in all three soul's hearts- a glow that was felt in the spiraling Cosmos.

CHAPTER 11

The Equinox Of The Fall
A Silver Lining

Juan Carless is up before dawn, out before his roosters. They respect him for this because they know he walks his beach front Casita yard and so the 'low-fliers' know he will rid any danger to them, such as, rattle snakes, coyotes, dogs, cats.. The lazy friers, they will get a bit of maize before being let out into the adobe-walled compound to spend the day foraging for the animalitas, and, Juan hopes, arachnids and scorpions.

Having done this, he enters his kitchen. It's an outdoor affair consisting of four vertical poles of 18" native California palm trunks about 10' tall and 4 cross beams of half split trunks 8' or so above the ground, the length that Juan's father could reach with his arms above his head. They are notched log cabin style. The perlins, or roof frame-work, is quarter split palm trunks on a pitch with woven-shingled palm leaves for the roof. There are nails, but mostly old lobster trap rope is used to bind it together.

He knows the water on the butane stove is hot and ready to pour over his coffee grounds even without his watch. The routine has been done even before his father. His two fishing partners shuffle in and three cups of strong Mexican grown coffee with sugar are consumed.

Juan is responsible for one of the Pongas in the fleet of fishing boats. There are 12 now in the co-op. They are owned by everyone in town and it is an honor to be in charge of one of the 20', 45 horse power out board engined open sea vessels.

There is much discipline involved here also. One example is; in case of high surf and or hurricanes, he must be aware at all times to secure the boats or move them to higher ground, off the beach, if necessary.

His truck, a white Lobo, has served him well. He bought it in La Paz 5 years ago and the co-op supplied him with a Ponga tow trailer. The trailer is no more than two 2"x6" boards nailed together as axles, with the wheels- 15" rims from discarded trucks or cars are mounted on both sides with large lag bolts. The width in between the wheels cradles the boat hull. A 20' rope is tied through a 3/4" hole drilled on each side of the wood axle, about 10" or so from the tires. (In the Pescadors language- as wide as an outstretched fingered hand.) This forms a handled loop to control the boat launch.

The Pongas are kept along the the sandy-shore beach, above the tide line, and are only trucked up to the village during increment weather. It is rare when a truck is needed, because, 3 men (Macho-Mexicans) can easily roll the axle down the sloping beach to the surf. The fishing vessel is balanced just off center.

It is an easy walk from Juan's Casita, but today he drives his truck. Maybe it was 'Waterman' instinct or maybe it was the groan in the ropes of the kitchen palapa as a stiff breeze caresses the palm frond roof.

A respected Pescadoro will put in 4 hours on the water and today Juan will be glad to return his Ponga to the beach when the Sun shows no shadows.

There is a cliff on the East side of the crescent bay and embedded high, maybe 60' up from the beach's sandstone cliff, and 10' down from the mesa, is a granite rock outcrop. And at certain Sunlight shadows of the day, there is a silhouette of a Tiburon to be seen. The Sun has not cast it's shadow on the beach yet, but it is glowing orange precisely above the shark formation.

But not as vivid as the neon safety-orange color of the fishermen's National-Mexican, safety-regulation-orange, hip-waders. They are issued to all 30 or so sea men. Fishing has been profitable as can be attested with the new gear, including new transceiver radios.

The launch of the Ponga orchestrates like this- With Juan's guidance, the boat is balanced between the wheels. The weight distribution favors the back of the vessel. The bow is faced to the water. Jose' pushes the stern and engine towards the sea and Edgordos mans the trailer from behind with the rope, using both arms and hands like a teamster. It's Edgordos task to steer and brake, while timing the wave-swell and direction of the Ponga in a perpendicular meeting with the sea.

A good timed launch rewards the crew with a bob of the bow rising over a waist high shore pound wave which flows under the keel of the Ponga, lifting the stern and engine above the wet sand and axle. At the first sign of floating, the Capitan leaps over the rail into the vessel, close to the outboard engine. Similar to a trick rodeo rider or circus performer leaping to the back of his cabello.

Jose' takes two steps out to sea on the opposite side of Juan and 2' in front of the Yamaha 45hp outboard engine.

With the ponga afloat, the teamster hauls on the rope and returns the home-made trailer to the dry sand, just above the high tide line.

But not this morning, for it appears that Edgordos has not fully recovered from a late night 'Barracho'. After an ill-timed loud peto-fart, the ponga was launched slightly sideways. The bow did not clear the incoming wave straight, causing a tilt and a splash that soaked both of his fishing compadres.

In retaliation, Jose' leaped in the boat chattering in Mexican, dark harsh words at El Barracho. Juan hand started up the motor and took the Ponga out in the water just deep enough to overflow into Edgordo's overalls. The weight of which unbalanced his leap into the boat and consequently caused him to totally submerge his body.

"You're lucky I don't use the Marlin gaff to pull you aboard," one of them said in the cacophony of ill mannered insults.

Four hours- though Juan wears a watch, their time is kept by the time it takes to motor out to the nets that are strung strategically around the bay and river mouths. They must body-haul in, pull fish, and return and secure with weighted buoys, yards of net. Then, return the catch to the fish cleaning palapa on the beach where they gut and fillet them. Fidel, the Beach Master and Mayer of the village, weighs and bags the pescos. The mostly sand bass are put into kilo sized plastic bags issued by the Mexican Feds, and are frozen in town. They are periodically picked up by a refrigerated Government truck and hauled to one of the ports along the Sea of Cortez and shipped to the Mexican mainland and sold.

But now, they must do extra, it is lobster season and there are 'longosa cajas'-lobster traps to haul in and reset, as well as the daily nets.

Jose', in his 10th season, takes the lobster hunt well. This is how Juan Carless understands and explains Jose' -

"He stands firm."

This is how that 'Red-Man' Ponga Capitan explains it to himself- 'Es verdad, es verdad."

Juan says out loud, "But I know he is thinking to himself.. Not too much work because I need my macho-virility for Modika."

"Que?" Edgordos grumbles.

Juan glances over in Edgordos direction, slightly, "Oh! Not you, I was talking to the Sea.

Edgordos likes this season..

"No mucho caliente del Sol, and Juan brings 'fumeairlitos'. And 6 bottles of cervesa."

"And, if we have 20 traps, each, with 30 Longosa! he has 1 pint of Mescal at the fillet palapa to share after the crew beaches and secures the Ponga."

Securing the Ponga consists of placing random found, personal, large angular rocks, heavy circular branched drift wood, or, prize-found metal anchors.

"Hey, you like your bath?" it doesn't madder who said it.

"Felt good. I don't use soap anyways. Now I must wear nothing until my shorts and t-shirt dry."

These fishermen don't use underwear unless their body necessitates the situation.

'Cha-Cha loco'- banter; all the same. It doesn't matter who says it.

"I know Edgordos hasn't washed all week." Aah-oh.. Broke the verbal spell. Too personal. Some one's name was used. Two against one?

Juan says, "if we don't do our work and reach the beach in six hours I will throw both of you overboard."

He could do it too. Jose' had thoughts about if Juan could.

Jose' is of good 'Red-Man' stock, ancient. In any tribe in the Pacific Rim, he could hold his own dignity. A case has risen concerning his respect. He has no children. In all civilizations in the Pacific he could have his choice of any prominent families' daughters, but this is a problem. In his mind and his worldly view, which is only as far as Mexico Highway-1. He resides 3 hours East or North, on a dirt trail through the Baja Desert that is barely wide enough for two domestic vehicles or one two ton semi truck.

The Tribe Aristocrats want offspring of superior linage, which he has, but, "I have failed to produce."

Juan comes from the first linage.. Ancient; with genes so strong, so intact, that after 10,000 years, his offspring still, all have perfect non-cavities teeth. All men are of the same physiques- perfect fisherman. Strong, stumpy legs, standing him at 6'. A muscular upper torso, especially the large hands. And skin as red as the bark of the California Arbutus and Manzanita desert bushes after a summer monsoon.

They are in a convoy. No order. In fact, the white churn off the back of the Ponga, caused by the Yamaha engine prop, has dissipated into the azure-blue sea by the time the next boat leaves the safety of the bay. The Pescadors like their solitude with the ocean. Will their personal Ponga wake send them to a good fishing day?

Juan swings the hand held throttle-arm a few degrees. There is a rusty roofing nail pounded into the transom and when the throttle-stick is in line with it, the boat will arc over to the Longosa sanctuary. Provided that the sea vessel's wake is in line with the granite Tiburon bolder embedded in the sand stone bluff.

Edgordos is mind-tripping on the foam wake, as it curls and twirls towards the Longosa lair. Edgordos is grateful for the rusty fat headed nail. He is grateful to work for some one so smart as to think of that navigational wonder.

The Japanese buy all the Village Co-ops' lobster and there is a strict rule that no one in town can sell the crustaceans. Shrimp are allowed for sale as are fish. It is also shrimp season and they come up with the nets and box-traps.

"Well, menos mal we don't have to set more traps for the shrimp," says Edgordos.

"No extra traps means sooner, I will be with Modika." Jose' is quite an hombre. "I understand that the shrimp are good for libido." He says to no one in particular, but maybe the Sea.

"Make you last long, and they taste good."

"How would you know?"

Aah-Oh, cha-cha loco broken! Edgordos is a virgin.

For 6 seasons, he has with this Ponga. Of a more refined stature, Jose' does not understand the old ways, or, maybe he cannot hear the music of the stars. He is one of the 'Second Comers'. This is how the Tribe understands it; "From after the big water," the Shamans say, "came the Clan that Jose' comes from."

"Yeah, and they taste good." All three have wonderful thoughts of a crustacean lunch. Each fisherman is allowed 2 regulation or larger sized lobsters for their families each day. There was a time when 2 could feed three people. And there was a time, 40 years earlier, when Juan's Father held one of these pinching brutes by it's claws, and, razing them out like Jesus Christo and up to his shoulders, the tail touched the top of the wet low-tide rock shelf that he was standing on.

He was free diving down in the submerged lava rocks of the area known as 'The Fingers'.

Civilization was different then.. Slower, the people knew everyone within a 100 mile radius. There were only a few families in this remote California Pacific bay. The desert palms were there and the cactus apples. The Gray Whales had been calving there for millions of years.

The whalers were there... there was no law enforcement, it wasn't needed then.

'Here' was 125 kilometers from any other settlement. A fisherman's shack was all there was in this remote bay, a 3 hour bumpy, slip and slide, dusty drive, south, from the village. It's still there as a town monument. A fresh water creek from the mountains ran to the Pacific Ocean within walking distance to the stacked stone hut. It is a 9ft, three paced, somewhat circular affair. A hand poured concrete floor was added later. It cracked on the first hurricane, which also took out the roof structure of palm fronds and drift wood perlins. The reason the floor failed, was because Juan's Father and his Pescadoro friends lined the floor with beach cobbles before pouring. A good idea; less concrete to load in the 1936 International 1 ton 'Dooley' truck, but, the sea-salt and minerals in the stones reacted poorly with the concrete cement, resulting in improper construction. Today, the dwelling still stands. It has adobe and cement walls that are crumbling, and it sits on 2 lots in a corner of town not far from the boat launches. When the Mexican Government got around to survey the lots for the village in 1959, the hut was found to be partly in 2 lots. The cracked floor is still there also. When the fishermen want Earthly solace with the Sea, or to remember their 'Tios', they still use it. It is far from being a shrine, but the town occasionally replaces the roof.

It was 1941. That was the year Juan's Father captured the huge Longosa.

The 'Fingers' was formed 2 million years ago. During the time of the great quakes. A violent rip in the Earth caused by the steady flow of the Colorado Granite Mountain river glacier melt during the ice age, eroded the sandstone low enough to explode the Earth's molten inner core to the surface of the Planet via volcanoes.

On this day in 1941, Señor Juan Carless has been staying in the hut for 2 days. He rowed his small, brightly painted red and blue, one man Nayorit-canoe from the village. A distance of 6 hours South from his salt and whaling town. He beached his hand carved craft not far from the fisherman's hut and unloaded supplies hoping to stay for 5 days and be back by Sabbath services.

The waves were there- Magical, unridden, rhythmic, perfect.. He was thankful for their lift to shore after the long paddle.

Señor Juan was alone. He had coffee, tortillas and beans, and cervesa. Enough for 6 days. The beer was tied to a rope and was dangled in a pool of sea water and mountain runoff below a waterfall which fed a large deep tide pool.

'Cervesa Frio' was a luxury only found in the hotel at the Cabo, a 3 day deep sand and broken rock shimmy-slide drive from this Bay.

At low tide, the lobsters were everywhere on the rocks. The young fingerling's, looking like so many bright red scorpions, were scurrying and foraging on the white sandy shore between 4 small, 200 yard bays divided by fingers of lava boulders covered with moss and edible sea weed plants. The adult's tail muscles were as large as the shin calves of a large, old school 'Red Babe', sitting.

Señor Juan noticed a large porous rock just off shore as he rowed in. On this day, he would dive under ocean to check for his prey. It was not necessary because there were plenty of easy pickings for the crustaceans on the shore rocks, but he liked the adventure.

An old, large, mucho patched truck inner-tube from a Bomack earth mover, used on the French copper mine in Mulege', was draped with an old discarded fishing net tied to the inside. It floated him and carried his gear out to the submerged boulder.

His gear consisted of a long 5' warn hexagon tire iron ground down on one side, the long straight side, as a sharp spear. The other side, being at a slight angle, the tool is wider here, was ground into a flat chisel-knife. It was good for scraping Abalones off the rocks. He also carried on the small bobbing raft a blunt military bayonet given to him by his Grandfather. It is of French origin assumed to be one from the Independence Revolution.

He left his sharp fillet knife on the beach, in the hut.

The water is warm, the sky is a clear Blue, and the sand is a Golden tawny-white, giving the sea, out to the rock, the color of Emerald and Jade.

The rock appears to the Red-Man as a thumb to the 'fingers' of the bay.

The boulder is large, it would not fit in the back of an earth mover. It is 6' under water even at low tide. To the sandy bottom is 12' and on the first dive Señor Juan realizes there is a cave through the center of it. He becomes totally fascinated with it, and, upon stalking this find, he does not notice the large pale-blue claw maneuvering behind the ancient lava and crystal speckled sea protrude. The rock is smooth and is the color of Cochineal-Crimson and Jade, very similar to the hue of the crustacean-beast.

He goes up for air.

He fills his lungs with oxygen.

On the next dive, he discovers that the cave is a tunnel all the way through. The bottom is paved in crystals of Jade and Quartz and countless small chips of inner Abalone shell. It appears to have a large enough circumference to fit a large Pescadoro. That is, one Hombre, in shape from spending 6 hours a day rowing and hand hauling nets.

Well, that is, except on the Sabbath, a good day for siesta in the shade. A good day for Reflection and Dreams, especially good, and bad, when sober.

There is also fiesta days which gave the hard working Pescadors a day or two off. And there are many, a wedding can last a week. On these days, that is, when cases of cervesa are shared by all, and it is good that these long fiesta days are few, for he would not be in shape to pass through the rock.

And then there are the 'Dias De Santos'..

Señor Juan was the first here and he was one Hombre in shape. Ah, a 'Macho-Man'.

The rock, 'La Roca', was formed during the time of the 3 volcanoes. The ancients, now the voices of the canyons and river mouth cobbles, say a huge ball of lava from deep in the Earth near it's core, was spewed from one of the moulting cauldrons rising from California Baja Sur. Not unlike a feline's fur ball hoarked from the Star Leo. As it rolled along down to the coast of the Pacific side of Mexico, an alley was formed as the Baja peninsula was ripped apart from the main land. This 'lava ball' rolled a distance of some 300 miles spewing out hot splashes of fire and essences of the Stars which then cooled leaving millions of stones scattered across the island-like desert. It leaped over the mountain near San Ignacio and landed with a splat in what is now a below sea level lagoon. And it kept rolling. When the lava ball came to the Sea, the great wind coming from the far North, from the Bering Sea, shaped the cauldron into a great pizza. The force of the hot minerals when they submerged in the ocean, created a phenomenon that can be best described as 'heat seeks cold, thus, motion'. The collision sent a wave around the world so fast that it returned in time to force a hole straight through the disk with a gigantic wave. The hole is lined up exactly with one of the Pacific Ocean's currents in a vortex, which passes through the large hollow to this day. It is, in fact, dangerous.

The Pacific Ocean has turned blue, not yet a Navy-blue, but close to the blue background on the flag of North America, as Juan comes out of his day dream. "The Sea is getting darker and the sky is puffing clouds in a swirl from the south".

"Yeah, they looking like the octopus," Says Edgordos, thinking he would like to catch one of the tentacled beings in the nets and having Chan-de make ceveche tonight.

Jose' is thinking, "A 'Chubasco' is coming, I will move fast and haul strongly."

"We will get or harvest quickly.. I think." He says out loud.

Thinking to himself, "Modika will rub my sore arms with the juice of the Aloe-Cactus and Marijuana's leaves tonight."

"Make sure that is all she rubs with that."

"You remember what happened with chili peppers.."

Yes, it is true, he fell for that trick thinking that it would make him virile.

Juan is day-dreaming again. He is thinking of the story his Father told him about the giant Longosa. He changes course an inch to the right of the roofing nail forcing the bow of the Ponga head on into the next larger forming swell. Soon the humming of the engine lulls him to his thoughts of fishermen in the past...

Taking a few shallow breaths, Senior Juan takes a deep one and shoves himself from the Bomack inner-tube raft and with the help from the weight of the tire-iron spear, he lands on the sandy bottom quickly. His Abalone skills were at work. He will have to explore quickly because his used diver's mask will not hold a seal very long. The mask is a vintage

French World War Two Cousteau-frogman throw away, and the rubber was not as scientifically pliable as todays synthetics are.

It is now, that the diver's attention on the rock noticed the tail, partially buried in the sand and small shells. It was as wide as a pelican's wing span, and was lurking on the backside of the boulder's cave tunnel. With closer inspection, the armored section of the tail moved into the cavern. The 'Pescadoro De Longosa' swam up for air, thinking to himself,

"The 'carne' on that thing must be as big around as my thy!"

The lobster knowns an intruder is there and has already stratigized his defense of the rock; with an all out attack at first sight of the Hombre.

The lone diver descends back under the Sea, with the spear point first. He notices the two claws protruding 18" out of the front entrance of the tunnel, also half buried in sand. "As big as Jaguar Paws!" He pushes off the sea-floor and glides to the surface.

The lobster knows the intruder had returned to it's realm and nervously fidgeted his 6 legs for grip and release among the crevices of the tunnel. The enormous Sea creature knew when the adventuresome stalker inhaled his breath and was coming back down.

Making a muted chop-chopping sound with the spade side of the iron weapon, the diver cleared the sand from between the joints of the partially camouflaged double-fisted claws.

The Longosa deflated his tail and pulled the two flukes together like a giant butterfly and then back like a diving sea bird. Creating a disturbance and diversion on the other side of the boulder.

As quick as he could pantomime a diving sea-lion, the weapon yielding man skimmed over the top entrance of the cave rock with his shirtless belly and blew bubbles into the crevice, stabbing the left claw as he passed. It was a direct puncture, rendering the clamping mechanism useless, but not destroying the claw meat. The iron spear ran clear through and then embedded itself 18" into the sandy ocean floor.

The Lobster withdrew it's weapons into the cave and was preparing for a backwards, tail first retreat, but found that his left claw was wedged outside of the entrance by the length of the metal bar. It pulled the iron weapon free from the sand and dragged the pole put it would not fit into the lair.

The diver went topside for air.

But quickly-

He knew he had to disarm and dismember the tail. A flopping fluke from a large, fearsomely clawed crustacean could slap and knock the Pescadoro over. Making him loose his breath. Maybe even break an arm! Or ribs! Even a bad bruise could make rowing back to the village unpleasant work. It would not matter, but he would have help to sanctuary with the current in his favor.

The Lobster's tail was exposed to it's extremely spiny vital cranium shell, away from the back of the ancient holed, lava projectile.

The conquistador-bladed assailant made his next decent into the now lobster-blooded murkiness. He straddle between the 6" spikes of which 3 ran along the back of the crustacean's shell head-plate. It was as wide as a trash can's circumference and, for a second, the move reminded this 'Longosa-Caballero' of the young black bulls he would ride for fun as a kid. Quickly, he plunged the harpoon-knife deep inside the underside of the tail muscle. The assailant worked the blade along the shelled cartilage sections forcefully, shallow, surgically, but not too close to the snapping, bucking hook projecting out of the top on the back of the shell.

In it's panic and pain, 'El Longosa Gigantor' managed to break off the useless left claw and darted from his lair backwards with Juan's Father gripping firmly with his bare legs. The diver, holding on to a spike with one hand, and the other hand holding fast to the duck-taped handle of the harpoon-knife, drove it deep into the beast between the thrashing tail and helmeted head.

The Hombre, still holding his breath, rode the dying creature around the rock one time. He went up for air.

Returning to the encounter, he grabbed the now unimpaled tire iron spear from the sandy bottom. With a backwards thrust, he pierced the Lobster just behind and below it's right eye. Then, leaping off the circulating crustacean, he spun around, holding tight to the head-embedded spear, he released the old French Conquistador bayonet from the beast. He needed air. He planted his calloused bare feet into the sand and lunged the spear metal bar deep and through 'El Longosa Gigantor'. Then he cut off the eyes protruding from the alien-like face with the knife.

A few more kicks of the six legs and it was over. The Pescadoro went up for air.

A hollow bump and a metallic scrape sound as the Ponga reached the buoys of the first lobster traps brought Juan away from his day dream. He had unconsciously slowed the Yamaha-engine down and all three Pescadors mindlessly went through their fishing routine of pulling ropes, hauling aboard the wooden boxes of traps, and sorting and keeping the large Mexican Federally mandated size, 'keepers'. Two in the first trap were put in the wooden fiberglassed holding tank located in the middle of the boat.

"Not too many Longosa." Jose' threw back 2 under sized ones.

"How you going to keep up your strength tonight?" Edgordos is over handing another rope-connected, wire-mesh trap. The side rocking of the Ponga as it rises over the South swells unbalances the over heavy Hombre.

"Stop that. You're making me sea sick."

"The hurricane swell is making them go deeper into the rocks." Juan maneuvers the vessel to face the bow towards the coming storm. "We better pull in all traps and take them to shore."

"The fishing nets can wait till after the squall," he said to himself.

They kept 20 lobster for the Co-op nets in the middle of the small bay. Bringing back a flotilla of traps drug behind the Ponga took most of the rest of the day. A longer work day than what is normal.

The wind and swells were picking up. It is at this time, 3 fingers to sunset, that the warm Chubasco off shore breeze delivered two old Surfers along side but 50 yards out to Juan's Ponga. They are expecting ridable surf.

CHAPTER 12

You've Got To Want It

A Surfer, especially one that has "Kahuna' statice, knows before a swell arrives. An old Kahuna feels it in his bones and joints. His knees, his hips, his arm sockets; all will give him a longing to stand up and surf. The old masters of ships with sails could read the clouds over the horizon and judge from the wind carrying them, the direction and speed in which a storm system was coming. And yes, certain Ocean disturbances return over and over, year after year.

With the onset of computers and Ocean wave signaling buoys, there are now a multitude of Surfers with a new, better, wonderful arsenal of knowledge for finding waves.

"Too bad they can't ride their boards as well as their knowledge. It will be a sad time for the Wave-Kahunas when they are no longer paying respect to our Planet who provides our swells", Red once said.

"They're coming!" Tex is on the computer looking for waves. He's been distracted by a series of adds that have been streamed into Cyber-Space. The Command-Center is located in a corner of La Casa del Poser. They call the cyber trans-receiver 'Captain Nemo's Command Center'. Buddy gave the electrical device it's name. ('Hal?')

He was found in the Cantina. He was alone, drunk, and obnoxiously loud, mainly talking to the hot-sauce bottles in the middle of the village made- stone, abalone shell, and poured cement, table. The worst problem was that he was annoying B'eme Jose'. Even though the Mexican, also 'Barracho', could not understand Frank's English babbling.

It was when the Vet asked for the Tequila bottle which was 1/2 empty, over the bar, behind Tica. He asked for two shot glasses. "One for him and one for the 'big' Mexican." That was when She sent Azul to fetch Slim or The Poser.

Dapper's Casa was the closest and he arrived just as Frank accidentally knocked his empty margarita glass to the floor. B'eme Jose' was thinking of cleaning up the broken glass fragments with the pretty-boy fireman's face.

Moving like a stalking, strutting seagull on hot sand, The Poser crossed the red adobe tiled floor quicker than a drunk can think. He stepped between the bar and table with his arms and hands outstretched behind his sides giving the allusion of gull's wings and squinted at B'eme. The Poser then pirouetted around 90 degrees, appearing as if he was a Spanish Matador and faced Frank.

"Hey, surfs up!" Dapper smiles like a Cheshire Cat.

That is the last Frank remembered of that day. He hadn't been remembering much for quite awhile.

"The Waves should be here in three days," calls out Tex. Frank is outside, on the shaded ramada, leaning on the palm railing overlooking the inside bay at 'Number 2s'. The new-comer Surfer is observing a seagull so white it appears almost transparent against the deep tropical-blue sky.

"This is Nemo's Command Center. We have located a Swell. Estimated arrival time- 72 hours," Frank absentmindedly says in a tone reminiscent of the dispatcher at his fire station. He is still tipsy from the night before and one of Dapper's Tequila bloody-Marys set him off.

"Correction, Captain Frank. Updated Command Center information.. Swell arrival time; day 3 at 0400 hours." Tex Ludie is using his Submarine-talk voice.

"Frank, are you going to be in town for the Waves? I would like to see that 3 stringer semi-gun of yours perform." Dapper has handed Tex Ludie his Chek Republic cut crystal tumbler with a concoction cocktail that, as he told Frank, will keep the Coyote that nipped you at bay.

"That would be a good thing to do. But, you know, I need to get to the hospital for my Amigos." And the old, now familiar darkness engulfed the Vet. "I'm leaving today, soon. I'll drive you to your dwelling Tex. Are you really that accurate with Nemo?"

"Six to eight feet and it should last for three days," was the reply from Tex.

Dapper clinks 3 ice cubes into his cocktail and steps out into the light breeze of just before noon. "The accuracy of Nemo?"

The Poser liked the name of the Command Center given by Buddy. "Come back and find out Captain Frank." He raised his tumbler and all 3 Surfers united with a light, controlled tinkle of glass and, looking into all 3 pairs of eyes, they drank a long spicy-hot swallow that burned from the throat to the belly. And they, all 3, roared with laughter as only Surfers can do.

In the distance, still hovering on the Ocean breeze, the Seagull erupts in it's lunatic cry to the wild.

When a swell comes, it is the ones that want it the most who perform. There are many 'buoys' in the salty lineup with the coming of the popular world class sport that Surfing has become. The average surf riders today are far better performers than the standouts of the generation before them. The 'Kahunas' in this age of Surfing still must achieve their status in the same way that is as old as time.

"One must live it, breath it, be a part of the Cosmic Melinue-completely." Red once said this.

It is the hesitaters, the ones doubtful of their performance, that will quickly succumb to the forces of Typhoon waves. Not all squalls will do this. It is the Hurricanes, some would call vicious, that will seek the true, complete wave riders known as 'The Kahunas'.

There is a difference, although slight, between those Surfers who truly excel, and the many who are just crazy, with no regard for death. There is also an exaltation of body, mind, and spirit that comes only after performing on one of the magic days when a Surfer becomes one with the Sea and chases and stalks only the biggest, grandest, and perfectly formed of set waves.

Frank bounced and rolled from side to side his 1966 Chevy 4 wheel drive 1 ton camper truck over bowling-ball sized boulders in the creek, flooring and chugging the vehicle's motor over the gravel bed of water still flowing, but lazily, 100 yards from Nat's Casa. Tex Ludie gave the closed passenger door a 2 handed drum roll and gave Frank the thumb in the ear salute. It is his way of signaling good bye. Nate would have liked the company now that his house partner, Red, was gone but he knew Frank needed to find his companions.

Frank was already into the dark trance which seemed to run his life now. He hardly noticed the devastation rendered from "Cochineal".

He found the statue of the goatee man with the bushy mustache on the esplanade in the middle of the two lane paved highway across from the hospital. The statue is of one of the Mestizo Revolutionaries of 1910. At the bottom of the bronze statue is a cement scroll which reads in Spanish the equivalent of "YOU'VE GOT TO WANT IT".

Frank had been at the fishing village (Surf spot) just 5 days and already he was feeling the laid back attitude culture shock from city life. Even here, as he parked in a civilized (large?) town in Mexico.

He walked through the glass double doors of the hospital and confronted Camilla at the front desk. He had in his possession the postage box of intricate parts for Buddie's knee replacement and places it on the entrance table. She gives him the slightly contemptuous look that only a Mexican woman can do.

"Señor Bombadero!" The only hospital orderly stretches out his hand towards Frank. They shake, "Mucho Gusto!"

Camilla's heavily colored eye lashes flutter and her blue-green lids flash. She adjusts her low cut blouse as if this Jock had been 'eyeing' her. "Senor Butmon and Senor Adam are in room twelve."

"Ven! Ven! (come), I will show you!" says the orderly.

The slap of his huaraches echoed pleasantly in Franks ears and the familiar sound of his gait gave Buddy and Adam a comfort. "Hey, I found this out in the desert. It has your name on it." The vet drops the box on Buddy's belly and then shakes hands like a man on purpose, with Adam.

"Hey, nice sandals. You get them from General Zapata?"

"Needs-foot oil, just like what is used on baseball gloves, that will make them pliable and stops the squeaks."

It doesn't matter who sad what.

"They're from Mazatlan. The Surfers in the village donated them to me. My white shoes were bled on beyond anything serviceable to a proper man."

Buddy and Adam smile big, along with Frank. The two look at each other and meet eyes. "He's changed," the eyes say. There is a spark in Frank's eyes. A spark that has not been there since long before his wife's untimely death.

A slight knock and Dr. Espanocha and his Intern step courteously into the room. They see the box but move over to the other bed in the room which holds the Pro Surfer. Dr Espanocha glances at the Vet's huaraches.. "Mazatlan, no?"

It's been 2 days since Dr. Espanocha set the Pro's broken left mandible jaw bone. The town dentist first removed 4 molars and in so doing, he was paid a share of the $10,000 pesos from the sale of Juan Carless's truck. The purple and red bruising covered half of the Surfer's face from the eye socket to the stitched chin, with the rest of the face swollen and colored an ashen-yellow.

"Intern, the sutures?" the Doctor pulls back the bandage. The Pro winches. The Intern quickly observes the jaw, stitched from the ear to the Surfer's Adam's apple and still smeared with small clots of dried blood.

The assistant's attention has wavered to the box with the artificial limb parts.

Dr Espanocha brow beats the soon to be Doctor and then, with a barley discernible smile, he says in Catalan Spanish, "Signor Denaldo Ortiz- I will take care of this. Will you please open the box."

There was a note- "Call Me Now." It was from Buddies artificial knee Physician. Intern Ortiz immediately opened his laptop computer and sent a text to L.A.-U.S.A.

The Doctor cleaned up the Pro surf rider's face and replaced his bandage. The Surfer still could not talk.

The Mexican Doctor and the Intern had all the parts and the schematics sheet out of the box on a special table that was brought in. Then contact was established with the L.A. artificial limb Specialist.

It was decided to do the parts swap the following morning at 8:00 AM and for Senor Denaldo Ortiz to study the Parts Assembly Brochure throughly.

The Intern arrived at 6:30 after studying the Manual until 10:00 the night before. Dr. Espanocha had been at the hospital since 5 AM, he too was now fully prepared for the surgery. Voice contact was made by 7:45 with L.A. Intern Ortiz computer could not establish Tele-Video communications with the hospital.

Adam and Frank left the room to get more money from the Banco De Surfen. The other patient had no choice but to watch because the operation was done in the bed next to his in the shared room, and no curtains. Both patients were heavily sedated.

"What's this-La Bombadero?" asks Adam as the Vets step off the high stone and cement curb into the now dirt street across which is the bank.

"El, Adam. It's El Bombadero." Frank chuckles and explains the horse-shoe tournament.

"Just like the abortion on Señora Vescahones pig." Said Dr. Espanocha under his breath at the finish of the surgery. He was supervised for 3 hours by the U.S. surgeon.

"What?" said the L.A. Surgeon from cyber space.

"Como?" said the Intern Denaldo Ortiz.

"A fine endeavor." Said the Mexican Doctor in Castillo Spanish.

"Send him back to the USA in three days." Was the advise from the Internet.

The hospital wanted 10 days convalescence before the 2 day drive to the International Border crossing. The surf-pro's insurance demanded he leave on the next available plane. That plane only leaves from the closest airport once a week which is on a Wednesday. That will be in 2 days. Buddy's insurance, the same one as the other patient, demanded that the portly Surfer be on that flight also. So did his wife.

An entourage of 2 vehicles, El Bombadero's camper truck with Adam and Buddy, and the load of camera equipment in the Custom, Crew-Cab Ford, 4wd truck; left the infirmary and drove the 2 lane paved highway 1, an hour to the airport.

It was a no-cloud morning with the tropical desert blue sky holding the dry heat of the radiating Sun. Juan Carless was hired to drive the custom truck, with the Pro, and the camera crew, up to the cargo door of the jet passenger plane. The equipment was loaded onto the plane.

B'eme Jose' had been miffed at the fact that he was not considered credible enough to deliver the movie equipment. After all, he shaved the night before. Every one in the village knows he only removes his 'begotas' once a week, on the Sabbath.

Juan was absent mindedly sitting in the air conditioned crew cab when one of the movie orderlies tapped on the driver's window, "OK" he said.

Juan electronically brought down the side window. He holds out the vehicles key fob. "Como?"

"It's yours," the man closes the Mexican Fisherman's fingers over the keys as a handshake. "You won the tourney."

Juan didn't understand all the English, but he understood that the truck was his.

"Adam.."

"Yeah?"

"Would you escort Buddy back to his wife?"

"Yeah, I can get a plane ticket. Are you driving home alone?"

"There's a swell coming. I think I'll stay and ride it." Says El Bombadero.

The eyes of the Vet's met and a smile from the heart that only Surfers know was created between the three.

"Nice truck.. It yours?" said Marina in her deep Californio spoken voice when Juan came back to the Surf village.

It would later be said in the small fishing town that the wager for the Pro's custom truck had to do with who will would get the most ringers. He wins the vehicle.

"Si!" and Juan hands a letter from the larger town's Post Office to her.

"It's from Tonga..." Marina tells Slim and she delicately opens it with her large fingers.

There are tears forming in her eyes. "My son is coming here for a visit."

Slim looks into her glossy, beautiful brown, Pacific Island eyes- "How many are coming?" in a voice sounding a bit more like the back screen door hinge of the Surf village bar than usual...

ENDNOTES

Thank you Mark Twain, J R R Tolkien, Herman Melville, Jack London, Tolstoy, John Steinbeck, Earnest Hemingway, Miguel De Cervantes, Carlos Castaneda, and many others for sending my mind away from TV in the evening and night hours of my youth.

And thank you for the illustrations Diez de Julio.

Printed in the United States
by Baker & Taylor Publisher Services